FALL FOR ME

Light My Fire Series

J.H. CROIX

To anyone who has walked through darkness to find light.

***Sign up for my newsletter for information on new
releases & get a FREE copy of one of my books!***

http://jhcroixauthor.com/subscribe/

Follow me!
jhcroix@jhcroix.com
https://amazon.com/author/jhcroix
https://www.bookbub.com/authors/j-h-croix
https://www.facebook.com/jhcroix
https://www.instagram.com/jhcroix/

Chapter One

PHOEBE

I stared at the text message, actually extending my arm and blinking at my phone before pulling it back into close vision again.

Phoebe, it's Archer Cannon. Remember me? Moving back to Willow Brook soon. I'd love to see you.

I set my phone down and crossed my arms, tapping my foot on the floor. *Of course*, I remembered Archer Cannon. He was one of my best friends in elementary school—those halcyon, innocent days that you could never recapture once the busyness of adulthood took over.

Archer had moved away after fifth grade, and I'd missed him so much. Standing from my kitchen table, I turned and crossed over into the living room area. Stopping in front of the small bookshelf, I fetched out an old photo album. My mother had made photo albums throughout my childhood, and she'd given me this one when I graduated from high school.

Flipping back to the early years, I found a picture of Archer and me covered in mud, standing in the mud flats along Turnagain Arm. Our rubber boots were muddy, and clay was smeared on our cheeks and arms. We held a bucket of clams between us with beaming smiles plastered on our faces. Another picture was taken on my birthday in second grade. Archer had helped my mother decorate the cake, and it was a disaster. I wasn't even sure what it was supposed to be. But once again, we were both smiling. We were almost always smiling in those photos.

I flipped forward to fifth grade. Middle school was weird. Some kids still seemed caught in the tethers of childhood, while others had growth spurts that sent them leaping ahead of their peers physically. Archer had started to sprout in height shortly before he moved away. In the last picture I could find of him, he was a good foot taller than me, and we were laughing while we played ping pong in my parents' basement.

Archer moved away from Willow Brook, and we stayed in touch sporadically, but this was before the era of cell phones, so our connection faded. I was older, wiser, and definitely more cynical than I'd been back in those days. I laughed to myself because it seemed strange to me that we'd ever become so close. My parents did okay, but we scraped by financially at times. There was lots of love in our family. Archer's family, on the other hand, was wealthy. Like seriously rich.

I didn't really grasp what that meant at the time. I knew he had more than we did, obviously, but now, I knew his family owned a sprawling international collection of businesses, one of which had been a mining operation outside of Willow Brook. His parents had run that portion of the family business. Their house was big but not too ostentatious, and his parents were blessedly down to earth and kind. I hadn't understood any of that when I was little. All I knew was he was one of my favorite friends, and then they moved away after the mine closed down.

I hadn't even thought about it lately, but the business name popped up here and there in the news. A legal fight was brewing over reopening that very mine. I wondered if that was why he was coming back.

Photo album in hand, I returned to the table, lifted my phone, and tapped out a quick reply.

Hey, Archer. I hope this is really you. I'm back in Willow Brook, and I'd love to see you. Willow Brook is still small, but it's grown a little. When will you be here?

Roughly an hour later, my phone rang, and I eyed it suspiciously. I'd already memorized the number where that text came from and knew it was Archer's number. I slid my thumb across the screen to answer. "Hello?"

"Phoebe."

The second I heard Archer's voice, my heart contracted. His voice had a rasp to it now, which was kind of sexy and a little weird. Butterflies flitted about in my belly. This was my old friend, and he was on the other end of this line.

"Hey, it's you!" I exclaimed, my voice pitching up with a squeak at the end.

"Did you doubt it was me?" he teased.

"Not really. We haven't talked in years, though. How did you get my number?"

"I still have your parents' number, so I called them."

"Oh, wow."

"I know. Moving away in fifth grade doesn't make it easy to stay in touch," he deadpanned.

I laughed, warmth spreading through my chest as my lips tugged into a smile. "So, tell me what's happening. Why are you coming back, and when will you be here?"

"Well, if you haven't seen it in the news, there's kind of a thing about my family's business there."

"I know. Are you going to be public enemy number one here? There's lots of local opposition to that mine reopening."

"Oh, I know. I'm trying not to be, but I'll be there dealing with the situation one way or another."

"And you're really moving here?"

"That's the plan. Tell me what's going on with you."

I filled Archer in on the bullet points of my life, both surprised and not at all surprised how easy it was to fall back into our comfortable friendship. I even told him the nightmare I was facing. It was mostly a nightmare to my pride, but still.

"He's a fucking asshole, Phoebe," Archer said flatly after I explained that my ex turned out to have been screwing around with my high school and college best friend from Willow Brook. Now, they were engaged and getting married here in town.

"I know he's an asshole, but it still sucks. Tasha even wants me to come to the wedding," I said with a weary sigh.

"I think you should go."

"What?" I squeaked.

"Absolutely. It sounds like she wants to save face by trying to talk you into forgiving her. Instead, if you're there, it'll be like waving a flag about what she did."

"She wants me to be in the wedding, Archer."

"Oh, well, don't do that. That's her trying to get you to sanction their cheating. That's shitty. You need to show them up."

"Right, and how am I going to do that? I'm a fire-fighter. It's not exactly a sexy career."

"It's totally hot. You're a badass," he said.

I rolled my eyes even though he couldn't see me. "I'm not a badass, Archer."

"I beg to differ, but we'll debate that later. I have an idea."

"What's that?"

Chapter Two

PHOEBE

"Archer Cannon?" Janet prompted.

"Yes. He's moving back to town."

Janet smiled, but it faded as she drummed her fingertips on the counter. Janet James was basically the spiritual and emotional center of Willow Brook, Alaska. She owned and ran Firehouse Café, the local favorite coffee shop, where I presently stood in line for coffee.

"Archer's parents are lovely people. Is he coming back because of that whole mess around the mine?" At my nod, she asked immediately, "What's his position on it?"

"I haven't gotten into that with him."

"That's going to be touchy if he's trying to re-open it. When will he be here?"

"Today. He's meeting me here for coffee, and I'm kind of freaking out," I said honestly. Because I was. It was so awesome to have Archer back in town, but I didn't know what to expect. There was also the matter of his proposed plan.

Janet smiled. "You two were besties when you were kids. Have you seen him at all?"

"I've seen his picture online. Don't you dare tell anyone, but I looked him up."

"Of course, you did," she replied with a shrug. "I've seen him too. That boy has turned into one handsome man." She waggled her eyebrows, and I ignored the flare of heat in my cheeks.

"I know. It's kind of weird."

"Let me get your coffee." Janet spun around to prep my order.

I was waiting at the counter when I felt goose-bumps rise on my skin and a sizzling prickle race down my spine. The chime on the door rang, and my body sensed this was Archer. Which made no sense because I hadn't seen him since the fifth grade. I couldn't even play it cool. I turned around immediately, a smile breaking across my face as soon as I saw him. "Archer."

His smile kicked up at one corner and then spread to the other, and those butterflies went absolutely wild inside my stomach. My breath became short, and my pulse fired off with the force of a rocket going into space. I barely had time to register his appearance before he stopped in front of me and tugged me into a hug.

Oh my, wow. An Archer hug, a full-on clench from this manly man who'd once been a fun, affectionate friend when I was a little girl. It was weird and discombobulating, and all of my cells felt as if they were sparklers spinning through my body.

He stepped back, his hands resting on my shoul-ders as I soaked in his appearance. Oh. My. God. Archer in fifth grade was funny, kind, and on the gangly side. Now he was something else entirely. His features were cleanly defined. His once kind of boxy-looking jaw was now chiseled. Was that the word I would use to describe my old childhood best friend? Yes, yes, it was. His nose was clean and straight, still a little big, but now that was sexy. His messy blond hair was darker now, almost amber with flecks of gold scattered throughout. His eyes—oh, dear god.

I didn't remember thinking about his eyes before. They were silvery gray, piercing, and intense. And his mouth? Gah! His mouth was sensual. His upper lip was narrow, accentuating his full bottom lip. I tried to take a breath, but my lungs had forgotten how to function, and I had to suck in air.

Meanwhile, he was speaking. "Phoebe, it's so good to see you."

His voice, which I already knew was kind of sexy, slid over me like warm honey. My belly was spinning in flips, and I was pretty sure I thought Archer was hot. It wasn't just because of his pictures online. This was no longer an academic, objective view. What the actual fuck was happening to me?

Chapter Three

ARCHER

Phoebe knocked the breath right out of my chest. Fuck me.

Okay, so I'd looked her up. Yes, I had. I knew, objectively speaking, she was beautiful. But seeing her again in the flesh was something else altogether.

This was not what I expected. Her blond hair fell around her shoulders, and her sapphire eyes were big. Her eyes searched mine, and her cheeks were a little pink. The urge to kiss her was fierce.

Holy hell. I had seriously underestimated my ability to manage this situation, and managing situations was my expertise. I was the problem solver for my family's sprawling business. I'd come up with a solution. It involved Phoebe and a technical deception, but I'd have to sort that out later. For now, I needed to get a handle on my body's raging reaction to her.

"It's so good to see you," I repeated, meaning it on a level I hadn't expected.

My old childhood best friend was still that, but she

was also beautiful and delectably sexy. "I'm getting coffee. Do you need to get something? Have you eaten? We should get something to eat," she said, slipping her hand through my elbow and tugging me toward the counter. "You remember Janet, right?"

Janet smiled over at me. "Of course, I remember Janet."

"Good to see you, Archer." She rounded the counter in a hurry, pulling me into a warm hug. This was the kind of hug, except for the mothering quality, that I had expected from Phoebe, warm and friendly and familiar. Janet's dark hair was straight, more liberally salted with silver than I recalled. Her brown eyes crinkled at the corners, and she felt comfortable.

"It's great to see you too," I returned as Janet stepped back and around the counter.

"I don't think you ever got to have coffee here. You were too young. Do you drink coffee?" she asked.

"Absolutely."

"What's your preference?"

"Something dark and strong."

Janet nodded. "An espresso then. Do you like it sweet?"

"Definitely not."

"What do you want to eat?" Phoebe asked, nudging me lightly on the forearm with her elbow.

That. That very gesture of hers was so familiar it caused emotion to rush through me. Back in elementary school, Phoebe and I always tried to sit together in class, and she poked me with her elbow whenever she was teasing or wanted to tell me something. Now, the subtle touch had a zing of fire chasing in its wake. That was *not* familiar. The sensation threw me off-kilter. Needing something other than Phoebe to focus on, I looked up at the chalkboard.

"Oh, wow. It looks the same, but I'm sure the menu's updated," I commented. Janet chuckled as she prepped our coffees. "Do you still have the sandwich I got when I was a kid?"

"A bagel with tomato and melted muenster cheese was one of your favorites," Janet offered. "You loved that and peanut butter and jelly."

"Do you still have that?"

"Of course, I do! It's popular with the kids. Are you going to get that for breakfast?" Janet teased as she handed Phoebe her coffee. "Yours is coming right up."

"I think I'll pass on the peanut butter and jelly, but I'll take the bagel with smoked salmon cream cheese. That sounds good."

"It is. I smoke the salmon myself."

"You do?" I couldn't keep the surprise out of my tone.

Janet rolled her eyes. "Just kidding. I don't have the time, but I get it from a local place, and it's excellent."

"Are you getting something to eat?" I asked Phoebe.

"I'm getting the bagel extravaganza."

"I don't know what that is. Should I get it too?"

"Are you going to eat two bagels?" Phoebe's brows hitched up as she looked up at me.

"Yes, I landed in Anchorage this morning after flying in overnight. I'm freaking starving," I replied bluntly.

Phoebe's lips twitched with a smile. "The egg extravaganza is perfect then."

"Would you like it with extra bacon and cheese?" Janet asked.

"Bacon makes everything better, so extra bacon is extra better," I teased.

Janet rolled her eyes. "Here's your coffee. I'll get your bagels over in a little bit."

Phoebe started to pull her wallet out of her purse, and I shook my head. "This is on me."

She opened her mouth to argue. "You can try to argue, but I'll just sneak behind your back and put something on a tab to pay for you in the future. Do you do tabs?" I asked Janet.

Her grin was wide. "I do. You'd better be good for it."

Placing a hand over my heart, I grinned. "I promise."

"I think your parents actually still have a tab with money on it," she replied.

"Are you serious?"

She shrugged. "Probably. I haven't checked in years, but they used to keep one."

I went ahead and paid for our breakfast and established a new tab under my name. A few minutes later, I was sitting across from Phoebe. I hadn't been lying when I said I was starving. A corner of my mind hoped that some food would cause this visceral reaction to her to dissipate. Maybe I was just so hungry I was misreading my body's signals.

No such luck. A while later, I had finished off my bagel and my egg extravaganza. Every time Phoebe met my eyes, it felt as if sparks shimmered in the air between us.

"It makes sense that you're a firefighter," I said as I set my napkin down on the table and took a swallow of my coffee, which was strong and delicious.

"It does?" Phoebe asked, lifting her hand and twirling a lock of her hair around her fingers.

I wanted to slide my fingers through her glossy hair

before I kissed her senseless. And that mouth of hers? Fuck me. Talk about a mouth made for sin. Her lips were plush, full, and pink. I could imagine just how they would look after a long kiss—swollen and kiss-bitten.

I forced my mind back to the moment. "Of course. You always loved to be outside, and you had more nerve than I ever did."

"I did not."

"Oh, you did. Remember that place we used to go swimming in the summer where the water was freezing? You were always first to dive off the rope. I had to get up my nerve to do it after you."

Phoebe threw her head back with a laugh. Fuck me, again. The sound of her laughter—raspy and throaty—went straight to my balls. Not a good place. I shifted in my seat, telling myself this attraction would pass.

"I do like my job. I don't even really think of it as a job. I won't be able to do it forever, but it works for now," she replied, hopefully unaware of my distracted state.

"What do you plan to do after that?"

"I don't know. I'll have to figure it out."

"You went to college, right?"

"Yup. I planned ahead and majored in wildlife biology."

"You probably have an opinion about my family's mine." I knew I was walking into a hornet's nest with public opinion about the old mine, but I hoped my plans would alleviate the concerns.

"Of course, I do. Not many people in Alaska want to see that mine open again. Is that why you're here?" Her blue eyes searched mine.

"Yes, but it's not what you think, which brings me back to my other plan."

"What plan?"

"The one to get back at your shitty best friend who's marrying your ex. See, if I'd stayed here, we would have been best friends in high school."

"I know." She traced her fingertip in a meandering circle around her coffee mug.

"Who is this Tasha, and how come I don't remember her?"

"She moved here in seventh grade. Her family is still here. That's why the wedding's happening here. I appreciate your offer, but don't you think it's a bit much?"

"Maybe, but it's not just for that. If I get married, I'll be able to take control of this entire branch of the business and shut the mine down. I'm thinking we get married the day before your ex-friend's wedding and then go as guests to hers."

Phoebe's eyes widened. "What?! Archer, that's insane. No one will believe it."

"Why not? We were best friends in elementary school. It's not like we didn't know each other before. We can totally pull off a whirlwind courtship. I normally don't care that my family tends to draw gossip, but let's use that to our advantage and completely show him up. We'll even make it a society wedding."

"Is there such a thing as a society wedding in Willow Brook?" Phoebe eyed me dubiously.

"We can make it one. Let's do it."

"It's just my pride," she said quietly.

"I know, but you can do me a favor and do something for the environment and show up your ex and your ex-friend all at once."

A slow smile stretched across her face. "You know what? You're right. It's totally worth it. I'm all about saving the environment and my pride at the same time. And we're friends. We can do this. I'm in."

Chapter Four

PHOEBE

"You're doing what?" Madison asked, her eyes going wide.

"What?" I countered, feeling my defensiveness rise swiftly.

Madison circled her hand in the air. "Can you clarify what you just said?"

"Archer's an old friend. He was my best friend when we were kids. I completely trust him, and he needs to get married so he can take over the mine and close it down."

"So, by marrying him, you're sort of saving the world?" My friend's lips twitched at the corners as she eyed me incredulously.

"I mean, yeah," I offered with a shrug. Madison was still studying me skeptically, so I pressed ahead. "And then I'm going to bring him as my plus-one to Tasha's wedding. It'll be a 'kill two birds with one stone' kind of thing."

Madison pressed her lips together, her eyes flicking down toward the table before she lifted her coffee cup, took a swallow, and met my gaze again. We were at

Firehouse Café because it was our favorite place to meet. "And you say you're not upset over your ex?"

"Well, I don't want the guy, but he cheated on me with my best friend, and that sucks."

I was starting to feel ridiculous when it all made so much sense when I'd talked with Archer about it. I'd even felt like I was doing something socially responsible.

"I get it. I definitely do. That is the worst kind of move a friend could pull."

"I suppose it's just about my pride."

Her lips curled into a full smile. "Well, you picked a good man to show her up with. Even I know who the Cannon family is. They own a massive conglomerate, and it all started as a small family business. I can't even believe they used to live here."

"Fireweed Industries started near Juneau, and the family owns land in Willow Brook. That's how they ended up here," I explained.

"Explain to me how marrying Archer will make it so he can close the mine? I'm a little lost on that."

"In order for Archer to take over management of this part of the family company, he has to get married. He plans to shut down the mine and reconfigure the operation entirely."

Madison blinked. "That is kind of cool," she said with another slow smile.

"I'm all about the environment," I said solemnly.

Madison sputtered on a sip of coffee with her laughter. Just then, the door to the café opened, announcing the arrival of Madison's boyfriend with a cheerful jingle of the bell. "Graham's here," I commented, gesturing toward the door.

Her head whipped toward the entrance. "Damn, you've got it bad," I teased.

When she looked back toward me, her cheeks were flushed. "I know." She shook her head slowly. "I don't usually get like this about guys."

"You sure do with Graham."

"Okay, before Graham, I didn't do that. Not even when I was engaged before."

"You were engaged? How did I miss this?"

Madison let out a soft sigh. "We broke up a year before I even moved here. Meeting Graham showed me I wasn't in love before. We had started dating in college, and he fit in with the life I thought I wanted." She waved a hand gracefully through the air.

Everything Madison did was graceful. She was beautiful—with glossy dark hair and pretty hazel eyes. She somehow managed to pull off that put-together look without seeming to put much effort into it. She was a stunner. Considering that I was a firefighter and prone to dressing casually, I could feel frumpy around her. Although I did know how to dress up when necessary.

"You wouldn't have liked me before," she finally said.

Cocking my head to the side, I gave her a long look. "It sounds like you just hadn't figured yourself out yet. That doesn't usually happen when you're younger."

"You think? You seem to know who you are pretty well. You went to college, you have good friends, and you came back home. You're a firefighter, and it completely suits you."

"I know, but it's not that simple. You were already in a career you loved before you moved here. Remind me what you call your job?"

"I'm an actuarian. It's a fancy way of saying an accountant who assesses risk. I did know my career path early, and I love it, but I was pretty shallow. My life had to blow up for me to figure that shit out. Anyway, back to Archer, have you seen him yet?"

I nodded quickly. "He's here in town."

Just then, Graham arrived beside our table, immediately putting his big palm on Madison's shoulder and leaning down to press a kiss on her cheek. She flushed again when she looked up at him. "Hey."

"Hey, how's it going?" he asked.

"Well, since I saw you half an hour ago, I drove to town, and now I'm getting coffee with Phoebe. She, however, is going to save the environment," Madison offered dryly.

Graham's alert gaze shifted to me. "Really? How?" A grin teased at the corners of his mouth when he glanced back and forth between me and Madison, who was looking a little too cheerful and amused by my situation.

"It's complicated, but trust me, it will work," I said firmly.

Graham chuckled. "Okay then. Well, I'm headed out to help Chase cut down some trees."

"Seriously? On your day off?" I pressed. "Are you guys working today?"

Madison laughed as she looked up at him. "Even when he's not officially working, he's working."

"Chase is planning to build a house, so I'm helping him clear the land," Graham explained with a shrug.

"Oh, good. I thought maybe you were secretly working, and I should be at the station."

"I'm not that kind of boss," he said as he shook his head.

"All right, well, have fun cutting trees," I offered.

"You two enjoy your coffee."

"Oh, we will. Also, we're getting drinks tonight, so

you're on your own for dinner," Madison said with a grin.

"Pizza, then," he replied with a wink. Graham was so enamored with Madison that even though he'd kissed her maybe three minutes ago, he gave her another lingering kiss.

I looked away, taking several sips of my coffee and waving when he finally departed.

"When do I get to meet Archer?" Madison asked.

"I'm not sure. We haven't worked out all the details. But he's around town, so you'll see him soon enough."

"Where's he staying?"

"At a hotel in Anchorage," Janet chimed in when she paused by our table.

I hadn't even known that but wasn't about to let on. "Oh, really?" Madison prompted.

Janet nodded. "He's airing out his family's old home and doing some upgrades on it. As far as I know, he's planning to talk to Lucy and Amelia about that. That house has just been sitting there all this time."

"It's been empty the whole time?" I prompted, surprised at this.

"Sure has," Janet replied. "They moved away, but they still own it."

"How old was I in fifth grade?" I mused.

"I think most kids turn eleven in fifth grade," Madison offered.

I counted with my fingertips. "I'm about to turn thirty. Oh my god, I never worried about being thirty," I said.

"Well, don't worry about it now," Janet offered with an airy wave. "Honey, I'm pushing seventy, and I promise the older you get, the better it is."

"You are not almost seventy," Madison breathed, her eyes wide as she looked up at Janet.

"Yes, I am." Janet was laughing as she walked off.

I looked back over at Madison. "I'm sure you'll see Archer soon."

"Well, the big question is, are you going to have to fake marry somebody unattractive?" she asked slyly.

"Nope. He's way too attractive if you ask me."

Just then, as if the universe had set out to prove a point, the door to the café opened again. Seeing as I had a line of sight, I reflexively glanced over just as Archer came walking in. Madison followed my gaze, and heat flashed into my cheeks.

"Well, well, well. Oh, my. No wonder you're willing to go for it. He is an eyeful," she said bluntly.

"Madison!" I hissed.

Archer's gaze landed on us, and he immediately veered in our direction. My belly swooped

Chapter Five

ARCHER

I'd had a good long talk with myself last night. Most of it consisted of trying to convince myself I didn't really think Phoebe was hot. And further, that my fiery reaction to her had solely been because I'd been starving and discombobulated after my overnight flight. It must've been a fluke because I hadn't seen her in a long time, and it stirred up emotions because she *had* been my best friend when we were little.

So much for that personal lecture. The second I laid eyes on her, my feet veered toward her as if she had a leash attached to me and was pulling me across the room. Except the leash was electrified and sent a current sizzling through me. She was sitting at a table with a woman who—there was no other way to put it —was stunning. I tried to focus on the woman with her—her dark hair, big hazel eyes, and nice manicure. All of it was a gorgeous package, and I felt nothing, not even the slightest attraction.

Stopping by the table, I risked looking at Phoebe again. The instant my eyes connected with hers, it felt as if my body was coming out of hibernation. Fiery hot prickles raced over my skin, and I didn't want to look away.

"Hey, Archer," she said with one of her warm smiles as she gestured to the woman across from her. "This is my friend Madison." With a quick glance at Madison, she added, "And this is Archer."

I looked over at Madison, dipping my chin in acknowledgment. "Nice to meet you. Phoebe's one of my oldest friends, so any friend of hers is a friend of mine."

Madison looked more amused than I would have expected. "Nice to meet you. I was just getting the news from Phoebe."

"Oh?" Considering that I had only persuaded Phoebe to go along with my plan yesterday, we hadn't gone over the details and whether or not we should discuss it with anyone. I wasn't sure if that was what Madison referenced.

"Archer?" Phoebe's eyes met mine. I saw the question there, followed by a hint of mirth. Phoebe had always had a sly streak. Apparently, she had decided she was just going to run with this.

"Yeah?" I prompted.

"I was telling her we were engaged," she explained.

"I think it's incredible. It's a love story." Madison pressed her palm over her chest dramatically. "Childhood best friends reuniting. I love it," she breathed.

"I know. It's amazing," Phoebe offered.

"When's the wedding?" Madison asked brightly, her eyes bouncing back and forth between us. She looked up at me, adding, "Phoebe didn't give me all the details."

No shit. We didn't have all the details. All I knew

was I wanted to make it happen before her friend got married. Glancing at Phoebe, I arched a brow in question.

"Valentine's Day," she offered.

"Oh, that's so romantic," Madison commented.

Janet appeared beside me. "What's so romantic?" she asked.

"Haven't you heard? Archer and Phoebe are engaged, and they're getting married on Valentine's Day." Madison eyed me with a sly glint.

Janet wasn't stupid, so I knew she sensed something was up, but she didn't miss a beat. She looked from me to Madison to Phoebe, back to me, and then Phoebe again before she pulled me into a big hug. "Oh, my gosh! I am so excited!" She stepped away. "You were such a sweet boy when you were kids, and you two were the best kind of friends."

When I looked toward Phoebe, she bit her lip. The second her teeth dented that plush surface, a jolt of lust sizzled straight to my cock. Fuck me. I thought this would be easy, but this was going to be hard in more ways than one. If I was going to convince my family, I couldn't do this half-ass.

"I love it!" Janet continued. "You can have the reception here if you'd like. Although..." She paused, her eyes arcing to me. "You might be a little too rich for this place."

"Absolutely not. Janet, you know my parents. They're still as down to earth as ever," I replied.

"I know, but I think you have a lot more money now," she offered bluntly.

I shrugged. I didn't like to talk about money but not because I hated money. My family *was* wealthy. Money could make things get weird and, on occasion, ugly, so I preferred not to let it define my life. "Phoebe and I haven't had much time to plan, so we would love to take you up on it."

Janet smiled. "One way or another. Maybe the bridal shower or something else." She paused when someone called her name. "I need to get back to the counter."

She squeezed my shoulders before she hurried away. Madison stood from the table, slipping into a fitted down jacket. "I need to get going. Why don't you take my seat?" She looked toward Phoebe. "I'll see you tonight at Wildlands."

Phoebe nodded. "You got it!"

I slipped into the chair across from Phoebe as Madison walked off. "I need to order coffee."

"I need to use the restroom. Tell me what you want, and I'll order it at the counter on my way back," she offered.

"A triple shot Americano. Can you order an egg extravaganza and a smoked salmon cream cheese bagel too?"

"Both again?" Phoebe teased as she stood.

"I like to eat. You remember that, right?"

"I do." She stopped, the smile slipping from her face. "I missed you, Archer."

I suddenly felt pummeled by memories. We'd had so much fun as kids. We were always up to something, whether it be tromping through the woods, walking on the beach, digging for clams, or fishing. All of it had been fun and easy. Now, I had proposed this crazy plan, and a part of me feared I might ruin one of the best friendships I'd had. I just hoped I could stay sensible.

"I missed you too, Phoebe," I said honestly. "If we

hadn't moved away before the era of smartphones and social media, I know we would have stayed in better touch."

She leaned over and gave me a quick and fierce hug. "I know. All right, I'll be right back with your coffee."

Her hair swung around her shoulders as she walked briskly across the café. Of course, because, apparently, I was *that* guy when it came to Phoebe, my eyes watched the swing of her hips and the way her bottom filled out her jeans so gloriously. She had transformed from a tomboyish girl into a beautiful woman. And she had curves, lots of curves.

The social circles I frequented lately in the city were filled with socialite types who tended to be so thin, I had to do a body check. Thin had never been my type, and it was downright disappointing. Phoebe was everything I liked. I was toeing the edge of danger.

Yanking my eyes away, I turned to glance out the window. Main Street in downtown Willow Brook was still quaint and familiar. I recognized a few of the businesses, but the area had expanded. The street was more crowded now, and there was an actual sidewalk. I didn't recall that from when I was little. Snow was piled up on the corners of the street and dusting the mountaintops in the distance.

"Well, hey there," a female voice said.

I glanced over just as Phoebe replied, "Hi, how's it going?"

The voice belonged to a woman with auburn hair pulled back into a ponytail. She was pretty in a practical sort of way. She smiled at me. "Hi."

Phoebe caught my eye, her lips curling at the

corners with a quick smile as she slipped into the chair across from me. "This is my friend Paisley. This is Archer."

Paisley's ponytail bounced with her nod. "Nice to meet you. Congratulations."

For a moment, I was confused, but then Paisley added, "Madison told me the news."

Phoebe interjected, "Thank you." She looked flustered.

"When's the wedding?"

Even though I was the one who somehow persuaded my childhood best friend to marry me, and the reasons seemed sensible, there was a wrinkle that unsettled me. I never thought I'd be attracted to Phoebe. Even more complicating, my attraction was like a brush fire set out of control and rampaging across the landscape.

Phoebe replied, "We think Valentine's Day."

Paisley nodded. "Rumor has it you might be upstaging another one."

"It's so romantic," another voice drawled.

I glanced up to see Beck Steele approaching the table. I remembered Beck. He was hard to forget. He was a flirt, even in elementary school. He'd been perfecting his craft in middle school. A small toddler held his hand, who I deduced must be his son since he was the spitting image of him.

I stood. "Hey, Beck."

"Long time no see," he replied with a chuckle, pulling me into a one-armed, back-slapping hug. "Good to see you."

"How's it going?" I asked as he stepped back.

"Life is good. This is my son, Max." He gestured down to the little boy.

Max eyed me curiously. "Who are you, and how do you know my dad?" he demanded.

"I'm Archer. I knew your dad when he was your age," I explained.

Max's eyes went wide as he absorbed this information. "Wow," he breathed.

Beck grinned. "You want to go to the counter and order?"

Max nodded vigorously, and Beck released his hand. "Tell Janet I want my usual coffee and an everything bagel with smoked salmon cream cheese."

"Can I have coffee?" Max asked cheekily.

"Absolutely not," Beck replied firmly. "You can get the kid's bagel and a hot chocolate of your choice."

Max sighed. "Okay, fine." Then he trotted over to the counter.

"Has he ever had coffee?" I teased as I sat back down.

"Of course not. You don't give coffee to kids. Maisie's gonna kill me because I'm letting him have hot chocolate. The sugar alone makes him wild sometimes," Beck offered with a wry grin.

"So, Maisie is...?" I prompted.

Phoebe chimed in, "His wife. Beck's a dedicated family man and totally in love with his wife. Who knew?" She lifted her hands and let them fall.

"Definitely not me," I offered dryly.

"So, you go by Archer and not Archie anymore?" Beck prompted.

I nodded. "Definitely. It's hard for people to take you seriously when you're Archie."

Beck grinned. "Aw, man, I like that name. How long have you gone by Archer?"

"Since high school. I can laugh about it now, but

you know, high school can be brutal. We had moved, so I was struggling not to be a joke to anyone. Anyway, congratulations on the family. Do I know your wife?"

Beck shook his head. "She moved here a few years ago. You remember Carol? She was the dispatcher at the station for years."

"Of course."

"Maisie's her granddaughter. Carol passed away, Maisie inherited her house, and Rex gave her the same job," Beck explained.

"Ah, well I'm sorry about Carol passing away," I offered.

"We all are, but I'm sure glad she brought Maisie here."

Phoebe grinned, leaning forward. "It's actually ridiculous. You weren't here for high school, but Beck became the most legendary flirt in town. I swear the guy would flirt with a rock. And then he fell for Maisie."

Beck shrugged unabashedly. "I'm still a flirt, although I don't flirt with rocks. That would be weird."

Phoebe rolled her eyes, and Beck glanced at me. "So are the rumors true?"

"What rumors?" I prompted.

"That you two are engaged. This is fast. If you two hadn't been best friends when we were all kids, I'd question it, but it's the real deal, huh?"

When I let my eyes slide to Phoebe, her cheeks were flushed pink. And just that, nothing more, sent another fiery sizzle through me.

"Am I invited to the wedding?" Beck asked.

"Of course," Phoebe replied quickly.

"Who's planning it?"

"Madison's helping," she said.

Beck grinned. "Good choice."

Paisley nodded vigorously in agreement. "She's the best option. I've gotta run. Nice meeting you," she called as she backed away.

At that moment, Max reappeared, handing his father the coffee and announcing, "Your food is coming."

"Thanks, bud." Beck grabbed a nearby empty chair by the back, swinging it over quickly and patting it. "For you."

Max clambered on it and looked around. Just then, the bell chimed at the entryway. Phoebe glanced over, and her eyes narrowed instantly. I followed her gaze to see a woman walking in.

I didn't recognize her, and then Beck said, "Tasha," just as Max announced, "You don't like that lady."

Phoebe's eyes shifted to mine. I hated the look held there. I believed her when she said she was well over her boyfriend, but I sensed it really hurt her to learn her friend screwed around with her boyfriend behind her back. Phoebe was the best kind of friend and didn't deserve that. No one did. I reached across the table, catching her hand where it rested.

"She's an old friend," Phoebe explained.

Max looked at me with the innocent curiosity of a toddler. "She must not be a nice friend."

Beck bit back a laugh, casting Phoebe an apologetic look. "Sorry, he's kind of blunt. He gets that from me."

"It's okay," Phoebe said, her tone injected with lightness.

Even though we hadn't seen each other in years, I could feel the tension emanating from her. I didn't like it. Tasha, who hadn't been here when we were kids, glanced over, taking in our table. She waved her fingers lightly, and Phoebe gave her a tight smile. She glanced at Beck. "Can you sit tight for a few minutes?"

"We're not going anywhere," he said easily.

I also remembered Beck was a good friend.

Chapter Six

PHOEBE

When Archer reached for my hand, the heat of his touch jolted me. He laced his fingers with mine and gave them a subtle squeeze. I took a breath. I was fine, I really was. It was just that what Tasha did stung. Big time. I'd trusted her, and she'd violated that trust deeply.

I was also unsettled because of Archer and my instinctive reaction to him. I sensed he felt my internal state. It was weird how easy it was to read him. And this attraction? Holy smokes. One hot fire was burning inside. Putting out fires was my actual job, yet with this one, I felt entirely powerless. My cells were aflame, and heat suffused every corner of my body.

Max was a great distraction. He looked up at me. "My best friend is Banana."

Beck caught my eye, mouthing, "Hannah-banana."

"How long has Banana been your best friend?" I asked.

"A long time," Max said firmly.

Seeing as Max was in first grade, it couldn't have

been that long, but in the life of a child, time was different. Archer's fingers tightened incrementally on mine again, and I glanced over to catch his small smile. It felt as if a ray of sunshine fell over us. He had been *that* kind of friend for me. It always felt easy to be with him. When I was little, I didn't remember life without being best friends with Archie. It was kind of funny how easily I had slipped into thinking of him as Archer, but it fit now.

With the distraction of Max and Beck keeping the casual conversation rolling along, Tasha didn't even come over to the table. For that, I was relieved. I knew she was coming back to town because she continued to email and text me and message me through other channels. The most annoying part of it all was she thought I was hurt about my ex. Oh sure, I was angry because he was an ass, but her betrayal hurt worse.

Max expounded upon his adventures with Banana when they went clam digging on the Turnagain Arm flats. It sounded exciting. I had done the very same thing with Archer more than once. Having permission to dig in the mud was a special childhood experience.

A while later, Beck and Max had departed. Archer and I were in the parking lot together. We stood beside my vehicle, a small, slightly beat-up hatchback. Archer glanced at my car and then to his, which was parked beside it. It was an all-black SUV and appeared decked out with all of the amenities

"You need a new car," he observed.

"No, I don't. Sapphire is doing just fine."

"Sapphire?" he prompted, his silver eyes glinting with humor.

My belly shimmied as sparks scattered through me. "Yes. Her name is Sapphire. She's loyal and reliable."

He eyed her rusty bumper and then the tires. "I forgot. Alaska doesn't even have an inspection requirement, does it?"

"No," I replied defensively. "So what? I have good tires."

"I didn't say anything about your tires," he countered. "Let me get you a car."

"Archer," I warned. I ignored the heat flaring in my cheeks. "I can't have you swooping in and doing all kinds of things for me."

"Why not? We're getting married," he replied matter-of-factly.

"You know what I mean," I ground out.

Just then, the door to the café opened, and I reflectively glanced over to see Tasha coming out. She made a beeline in our direction. "Fuck, Tasha is coming over," I muttered.

"Perfect," Archer said confidently.

Before I could even ask why that was perfect, he closed the distance between us. Sliding an arm around my waist and dipping his head, he murmured, "I'm going to kiss you."

I opened my mouth to protest, only to have his lips land on mine. I was surprised lightning didn't bolt into the sky from where our lips touched. The sensation sizzled through me, fire spinning in my veins. I should've protested, but I was in shock. I promptly discovered Archer knew how to kiss. Holy hell.

His lips brushed over mine, once and then twice, soft but firm at the same time. He whispered against my mouth, "Hold on, Phoebe."

His fingers slid through my hair as he cupped my nape. His touch sent tingles chasing down my spine and radiating everywhere. When his tongue swept into my mouth, all I could do was gasp and shamelessly moan. My tongue was teasing against his because I couldn't help it. This was all fake, but it wasn't. Then again, it was, and I didn't even know what to do.

The only thing that made sense was to kiss him back, or at least that was what my body thought. By the time he lifted his head, I didn't even know how much time had passed. I was gobsmacked as I stared up at him, gulping in ragged breaths of air. My pulse thrummed.

Just then, I heard Tasha's voice. "Wow. I heard you two were engaged, but I wasn't sure if it was just a rumor."

Archer kept his arm around my waist as he turned to the side, facing her. "Excuse me?" His tone was crisp and haughty, a side of Archer I'd never seen.

I flapped my hand in her direction. It was a damned miracle I could even move. "This is Tasha. We were friends in high school."

"Oh, the shitty best friend who cheated with your ex-boyfriend, the asshole," Archer stated, glancing at me.

I nodded. Because it was all true. "Yeah. We broke up for other reasons before I found out," I added.

Archer looked back at Tasha. "Phoebe and I were best friends all the way through fifth grade before you moved to town."

Tasha's eyes narrowed, her lips pressing in a line, as her cheeks flushed a splotchy shade of red. "You don't understand."

"Sure I do," Archer replied easily. "It's pretty straightforward. Don't fuck your friend's boyfriend."

"They broke up anyway," she ground out.

"So? Now you want her to be in your wedding."

Tasha lifted her chin. "We were friends. I understand she's a little put out."

"I didn't love him, Tasha. That was never the point. I just thought you were my friend."

"We'll be at your wedding now," Archer said.

Tasha stuttered. "Wh-why, what?"

He shrugged. "It'll be one of those let bygones be bygones things. The only way to earn forgiveness is to own it, so own it."

Tasha blinked. "Um, okay. When is your wedding?" she asked next.

"Valentine's Day. We thought it'd be romantic. We've known each other forever, so we don't see any reason to wait long," he replied.

Tasha's eyes flicked back and forth between Archer and me. I knew my former friend well. She was furious. Weddings had always been important to her but not so much to me. She smiled tightly.

"We already have your address. Invites are going out next weekend. We hope to see you there. Please bring your fiancé," he said smoothly.

"Okay. Bye." She turned and stalked across the parking lot.

Archer looked down at me. I still hadn't recovered from our kiss. Little eddies of sensations swirled inside.

"How are you doing?" he asked, a sly glint in his eyes.

"You are *good*," I finally said.

He grinned, and my belly somersaulted as I tried to take a breath. I was in trouble. *Big* trouble.

Chapter Seven

ARCHER

I sat in my SUV, staring at my childhood home. My body was still reverberating from that kiss with Phoebe. Fuck me. That kiss had been strategic, or so I'd thought when I started it.

I was pissed off at Phoebe's friend. What the fuck? She was an awful friend. My anger was righteous, yet I'd made a significant miscalculation. I had deeply, and perhaps disastrously, underestimated my attraction to Phoebe.

"Shit," I muttered to myself.

My plan made sense. Get married, inherit this branch of my family's sprawling business, and shut the mine down. "Yay for the environment." I laughed to myself as I leaned my head back.

To the day, Phoebe was the best friend I'd ever had. Our marriage would make her ex look like the asshole he was. I believed her when she said she was over him. But I knew how much friendship mattered to her. I knew how much it hurt her that her friend had screwed around behind her back. What a fucking bitch.

I was jolted out of my train of thought when my phone rang. I hadn't even turned off the engine yet. That was how out of it I was after that kiss. So much for thinking I had it all under control.

The phone rang again, and when I saw my mother's name flash across the screen, I tapped it. "Hey, Mom, what's up?"

"Archer. How's Willow Brook?"

"It's beautiful. I just pulled up to the house, in fact."

"Oh wow. Have you been inside yet?"

"Just for a few minutes yesterday. It's like walking into a time warp," I said dryly. "How come you and Dad never came up here after we moved away?"

"We did a few times, but then life kept us busy. Enough on that, though. Is your news true?"

"What news?" I countered even though I knew precisely what she was asking about.

"You know what I mean," my mother chided. "Are you engaged to Phoebe?"

I chuckled. "I do know what you mean, and yes."

"Oh!" My mother let out a little sigh. "I *love* this. You two were such good friends when you were little. I don't think you've had a friend like her since then."

"I haven't," I agreed.

"Please give her my best. I'm thrilled for you both."

Although my mother might be suspicious, she'd always had a soft spot for Phoebe. She'd also bemoaned my lack of romance of late.

"You can tell her yourself. You're coming to the wedding, right?"

"Of course! Is it soon?"

"We're planning for Valentine's Day."

"Wow, you're not wasting time."

"Definitely not. Maybe we're new as a couple, but we've known each other forever."

"So true. How many people are you inviting?"

"Well, family is welcome. Phoebe will invite her family and friends. I'm guessing it will be on the smallish side, though. Willow Brook is still a small town, and I don't suspect many people will make the flight up here."

"We'll see," my mother replied lightly. "Since you're getting married, you'll be taking over the reins for that side of the business. Dare I ask what your plans are with the mine?"

"I'm shutting it down," I said flatly.

My mother let out a laugh. "I think that's great. I do wonder what Clint is going to think about that," she said, referring to my great-uncle who'd been managing this part of the business for years.

"I don't really give a shit what he thinks."

"Do you think he'll doubt the marriage?" she asked.

"No. The marriage is real. I've known Phoebe longer than just about anyone other than family. The business part is secondary."

The odd thing was when I hatched my plan, the reverse was true. I'd seen an opportunity and angled for it. Now, I was already falling for Phoebe. It wouldn't be fake to show how much she meant to me.

Our old friendship was a foundation. I knew her and trusted her in a way I didn't trust anyone, except for maybe my parents. When I'd seen her pictures on social media over the past few years, of course, I'd noticed she was beautiful. But that was more of an objective perspective. Nothing could have predicted the fiery chemistry that sizzled between us. And that kiss? Fuck me.

I was losing control of the narrative much faster than I could ever have anticipated. I heard the sound of tires on gravel and glanced over my shoulder to see a vehicle with Kick*** Construction emblazoned on the side of it.

"Hey, Mom, the construction crew I'm talking to about updates just got here. I'm going to let you go. Tell me when you'll be up here, and I'll make sure the house is ready in time."

"We'll be there probably a few days before the wedding if that's okay."

"Of course, it's okay. I love you."

"Love you too, Archer. Give Phoebe my best and tell her we can't wait to see her. We're thrilled she's going to be part of the family."

"You got it."

I hung up the phone and stepped out of the SUV. Amelia Masters was approaching from the truck. Tall and leggy, she flashed a smile. "Hey there, Archer. I hear you go by Archer now."

"I do." I gave her a quick hug before stepping back. "Long time no see."

"Definitely. Congratulations on your engagement to Phoebe. I think it's awesome," Amelia replied.

She seemed sincere and not even the least bit doubtful.

"I think it's awesome too."

She nodded firmly. "Absolutely. You two were besties growing up. It fits."

"And you're married with a kid?"

Amelia's cheeks flushed slightly as she shrugged. "I know. It's crazy how much life changes. Cade and I started dating in high school, then we broke up. It was kind of dramatic."

"You seem to be all settled now," I replied.

She grinned. "We are. Life is good."

Another truck came down the drive, and a moment later, a petite woman with blond hair who resembled a fairy climbed out. She barely reached Amelia's shoulder. Amelia was on the tall side, almost as tall as me.

"This is Lucy. She's my best friend, and we run the construction company together," Amelia explained. "Now, let's get down to business. What do you need?"

"Rumor has it you're the best place in town, and you're busy. I'm willing to pay extra if you can do some updates on a tight deadline."

Lucy eyed me skeptically. "You're rich. How quick and how much do you want done?" she asked bluntly.

I chuckled. "Mostly, I want the master bedroom and bath updated quickly. For the rest, you can take your time."

Amelia rested a hand on her hip. "We're a small crew. That's how we keep quality up. So, you're either going to be patient or find another company. I can make some recommendations from Anchorage if you'd like."

I shook my head. "Nope, I'll be patient."

Lucy wrinkled her nose as she looked up at me. "We can probably squeeze in the two rooms early. Let's take a look."

"The bones are good, I promise," I said as I led them into the house.

A short while later, they left with a plan, and I set up a deposit to be wired over to their account. To get started, they thought they could have the updates done on the bedroom and bathroom within a few weeks. They gave me the name of a furnishing place in Anchorage. The one thing my parents had wisely done was take everything out of the house. They told me they'd left some boxes in storage in the garage attached to the guest house. I headed over there to take a look around. Aside from finding some old kitchen items and papers from the business, I found an old photo box that was left behind by accident.

I ended up sitting on the floor with my back against the wall as I flipped through a photo album from my elementary school years. There were plenty of photographs of Phoebe and me. We'd spent so much time together then. My heart gave a peculiar twist as I laughed softly, looking down at a picture of us digging for clams on the Turnagain Arm flats. Both of us were smeared in the mud. Phoebe's blond hair was pulled up in a ponytail, hanging lopsided on her head with a wide smile wreathing her face. Another picture was of us holding hands as we jumped up and down in a puddle. The water splashed around us, glittering in the sunlight and leaving splotches on the photos from the lens.

I closed the photo album, thinking of her now. My mind flashed to the feel of her lips underneath mine. Heat sizzled through me, and I stood abruptly. I'd meant to just go through the motions of the marriage yet somehow not make it official. But my mother's comment about Clint reminded me I'd better make it official or my great-uncle would cause trouble. He was a fucking asshole.

Chapter Eight

PHOEBE

A few weeks later

"You mean move in here?" I asked, my voice rising to a squeak with the last word.

Archer's eyes never left my face, and his lips twitched at the corners with a smile. My belly spun in dizzying flips. Butterflies took flight, sending tingles through my body.

"Yes," he said simply.

It made sense logically, and I knew that. We were going to get married.

"Um, okay. How far away is Valentine's Day?" I asked.

"Two weeks. How's the wedding planning going?"

I took a quick breath of air, gulping it in almost too fast. I felt a little light-headed from the rush of oxygen. "It's going. We'll be at the church. When is your family coming to town?"

"My parents will be here a few days beforehand, and hopefully a cousin or two. I'm not sure yet."

I nodded, feeling a little crazy inside. "It'll be nice to see them."

"They're excited to see you. I was just talking to my mom this morning. She said to give you her best. I think we should go out for dinner in town soon."

"Dinner?" I prompted slowly.

"Yeah, you know, that meal people have. We could call it supper. Dinner is technically lunch, or it used to be in England."

"Yes, we should, we should." Why was I repeating myself? Gah!

"We need to be seen in public. Rumor has it Tasha's fiancé has arrived in town."

"You heard that?"

Archer nodded, and I stood there, feeling ridiculous.

He reached out and put his hands on my shoulders. "Phoebe, it's fine. I know you're over him."

"Yeah, I just feel stupid, you know?"

"Well, yeah. I'd feel stupid if my ex was with my best friend. My point being, I think I get that you're more upset about your friend. You're a really good friend, and it's her loss. After meeting Tasha, my sense is she wishes she could fix it. I'm guessing you want to fix it for her, but you can't."

I took a breath, trying to steady myself inside. "I know she does, but she can't undo it."

Archer cocked his head to the side, studying me quietly, and I suddenly realized he knew me better than anybody. "You could let it go. She's not worth it."

"Maybe after my pride feels a little better." I lifted my chin slightly.

His lips kicked up at one corner in a half-smile, sending my belly into a tizzy. "Well, you have better things to do."

"Like marry you and save the planet, or at least a river and the salmon run," I teased.

He laughed, the sound deep and gravelly. It rumbled through me, and I loved the way it sent a little shiver over my skin. His hands were still on my shoulders, and we stared at each other. We were alone in this house that, apparently, I needed to move into. Our wedding night was only two weeks away.

"Where are we going to sleep?" I blurted out. We were standing in the empty bedroom, which Amelia and Lucy had finished updating already.

Archer's eyes never left mine. "I hired a place in Anchorage to furnish it. I was actually hoping you'd join me when I talked with them, so we could pick things out together. Does this afternoon work?"

"I guess."

"They're coming here, so we don't have to drive anywhere. Are you okay?"

His hands fell away from my shoulders as he stepped a little closer. His palms slid down my arms, gripping my hands lightly.

My heart felt like a rabbit racing madly in my chest. I stared up into his gray eyes, trying to remind myself he was my old friend, Archie. Just my absolute favorite childhood friend. We did the goofiest stuff together. I never, absolutely *never* ever, thought I might think he was sexy.

Trying to reconcile *this* Archer with the Archie I knew when we were little was challenging. Yet the comfort and familiarity I felt with him were still there. It came so easily. I didn't even have to think. We slipped into our old friendship, except there was this wildly inconvenient chemistry, and then he'd gone and kissed me. I couldn't forget it and had probably replayed that kiss hundreds of times in the hours afterward.

Now, he wanted me to pick out furniture with him and stay with him. Oh. My. God. I didn't know what I'd been thinking when I said I would do this. I really didn't even care about my ex. What an asshole. And my shitty friend, Tasha.

I couldn't break away from Archer's gaze. Heat bloomed under my skin, and my cheeks got hot as I stared up at him. I cleared my throat and licked my lips, trying to remind myself he was a billionaire with lots of money. All he had to do was get married, and then he could shut down that mine project. It was good for the environment.

"Phoebe?" he prompted.

Oh, right. He'd asked me if I was okay.

"Yeah," I finally managed.

"What's going on in your brain? You're thinking really hard."

I knew I could come up with something flippant and dismissive. Surely, I could. Instead, like a complete idiot, I blurted out the worst question ever. "Why did you kiss me?"

His silver-smoke eyes searched my face, and I felt as if he could see right into my heart, opening the doors and peering inside. I shifted on my feet, and butterflies twirled in my belly, tickling and sending sparks in a fiery scatter through me.

"I could lie and tell you it was because I wanted to make Tasha know we were for real, which is true. That isn't a complete lie, but I also wanted to kiss you. Is that a problem?"

I took a breath, trying to kick my brain into gear. Then he added, "I *really* wanted to kiss you."

Oh, my god. My heart went crazy, racing at the

pace of a cheetah. My chest felt like it was going to crack open from the thundering beat. I could hardly get a breath, and my belly was spinning as heat slid through me in a fiery shimmer.

"You wanted to kiss me?" I rasped.

His eyes darkened as he nodded slowly. I knew this guy had way more experience than me with dating. His family had money, serious money. He'd probably dated models, and I was his old friend who was a firefighter and favored jeans and boots over dresses.

"Did you want to kiss me?" he asked, each word deliberate and slow in that husky, purposeful voice of his.

I seriously thought I might melt to the floor. I wanted to somehow be someone I wasn't—cool and calm like I could handle this smoothly. It was a lost cause, just like my panties. Staring up at him, I felt my head nodding as I whispered, "Yes."

I had no idea how long we stood there, but it felt as if we were caught in some kind of strange hot shimmering space. My heart kept on racing, and air was hard to come by.

Archer's eyes were dark. I didn't even think of him as Archie anymore. He was a man, he was Archer, and he felt like mine.

"Well, then," he finally said. "I think we should try again. Practice makes perfect, right?"

My heart turned over. He released one of my hands, his fingertips dusting across my forehead as he brushed my hair back. His hand slid through the locks, and I could feel every touch. My senses were attuned to him and only him. The pads of his fingertips were warm and dry as they brushed along the base of my skull. The subtle sensation of his breath as he dipped his head and dusted a kiss on the side of my neck caused me to tremble, shivering all over.

I heard myself whimper and was instantly shocked. I was not *that* girl. I didn't get all breathy and whimper about anyone. In fact, that was one of my ex's complaints. I was too tough. He wanted someone more feminine, or that was what he'd said in one of our arguments. Thank God I'd been the one to dump him first.

None of those thoughts tumbled through my mind at this moment, though. None at all. With Archer, I felt entirely feminine.

He lifted his head, his eyes catching mine like a beam. I couldn't look away. I trembled again, sucking in a quick shuddery breath. I thought he was going to bring his lips to mine. I craved it. I was impatient for it. All of me was leaning up toward him.

He had so much more control than me at this moment, *so* much. He dipped his head again, dusting a kiss on the other side of my neck, and I let out another whimper. He released my other hand, his palm sliding around my waist. His fingers angled down over my bottom but not far enough. His hand slid through my hair again, and he palmed my cheek. Then he dragged his thumb across my bottom lip, and I thought I might burst into flames from the heat searing me inside. My mouth parted, and I swallowed as I frantically tried to think. My brain cells had immolated. All I could do was stare at him as my heart beat out his name against my ribs.

"You are so gorgeous, Phoebe," he murmured.

That snapped through my awareness, sending a jolt of insecurity through me. I was shaking my head before I could even think. His eyes narrowed. "What? You don't get to disagree with me."

I pressed my lips together. His thumb was still there, resting just below the center of my bottom lip. "I'm not gorgeous. I'm a tomboy. I'm a firefighter."

"So, what if you're a tomboy and a firefighter? You're beautiful, and you're my best friend. I'm so glad I found you again."

I was trying to absorb all of that when he added, "I want to kiss you now, so shut up."

I was stunned at his words, so stunned that I did, in fact, shut up.

His hand fell away, and he made some kind of sound, almost a growl, as he dipped his head. His lips brushed over mine once and then again before he angled my head to the side and fit his mouth over mine, claiming our kiss.

I gasped into his mouth when his hand slid down over the curve of my bottom. He just barely nudged his hips into mine. I was almost shocked at the feel of his arousal, hot and thick against me.

Archer kissed like a master. He alternated with commanding sweeps of his tongue before gentling and drawing back into a lingering kiss. He nipped, he dropped hot kisses at the corners of my mouth, he pressed open kisses on my jawline, and all the while, I melted. It felt like a dance, a push and a pull, and I just kept falling deeper and deeper. By the time he gentled our kiss and broke away, I was clinging to him with one arm banded around his waist and the other clutching his shoulder. His muscled shoulder, of course. I was plastered against him. My nipples were tight and achy, and I could feel the wet silk between my thighs.

I blinked up at him. "Oh."

The only relief for me was Archer looked as stunned as I felt. The sound of the doorbell echoed from the front to the upper floor. With the house empty, the sound carried easily.

He didn't move for several long moments as he stared at me. His palm moved in a smooth caress from my bottom and up my spine. He pressed his lips to mine once more in a lingering kiss just as the doorbell rang again.

"That'll be the furnishing team," he murmured.

Chapter Nine

ARCHER

I tried, I *really* tried to stay focused. I prided myself on having an impenetrable professional demeanor. Phoebe had shaken me. Well, not Phoebe. Kissing Phoebe and kissing Phoebe again had shaken me to my core.

Phoebe was my old friend, but she was so much more. I wanted her, and I didn't want this marriage just to be fake. Meanwhile, the interior decorator was rambling on about something. Phoebe looked a little dazed, and I smiled to myself at that. I was dazed. At least it wasn't just a me thing.

"What do you think?" the woman said. I couldn't even remember her name at the moment.

"I think unless Phoebe has a preference, I'm willing to let you make the call."

The woman shifted her attention to Phoebe, and Phoebe looked at me. We looked together at the woman, and I almost burst out laughing.

"I don't like bright colors in the house," Phoebe finally said. "Maybe something subtle with, I don't know, neutral shades."

"Neutral is the way to go for background, and if you want to add touches of color, you can do that with artwork. I'd recommend a comfortable, modern vibe. This house calls for that," the woman explained.

"It's my parents' old home, so I want it to be something they would like. Neutral colors will work for that," I heard myself saying.

"Will you be living here full time?" the woman asked.

I reached for Phoebe's hand, lacing my fingers in hers and giving it a little squeeze. "We haven't made all those decisions yet. We will definitely be here part time," I explained, hoping Phoebe wouldn't start to get antsy.

Phoebe aside, I'd already considered staying here. Willow Brook felt like home to me because it was where I'd grown up.

I could work here easily. With the internet and online cloud storage, I could work anywhere. I could travel for meetings. But I knew it would freak Phoebe right the hell out if we jumped to that today.

We still had to get past the kisses, and I had to convince her that we could do more than kiss.

Oblivious to my mental machinations, the woman continued, "Well then, how about I come up with some ideas and sketches? I can send them over online."

"Sounds perfect," I replied.

Phoebe and I walked her to the front door, and the woman left. The sound of the closing door echoed in the space. I turned and looked around. I loved this home. It was where I grew up.

The downstairs was all hardwood flooring, except for the tiled kitchen. It was an open space with a vaulted ceiling and exposed beams. The main room had windows in the center and two walls of windows flanking the sides. The kitchen was to the back, and the upper floor was only half of the house with a balcony hallway on the side. The main bedroom was on one end upstairs with three smaller bedrooms along the balcony.

Phoebe looked up at me. "How does it feel to come back?"

When I met her eyes, my heart stuttered and then lunged. I forced myself to ignore my internal state. "Good, really good, actually."

She squeezed my hand. When she smiled, for just a second, I saw the little girl I'd known all the way up through middle school. She had a dimple that sometimes showed in her right cheek. It peeked out just now. My heart flipped in my chest.

"It's really good to see you again, Archer."

"Same," I said gruffly.

"Are kisses complicating us?" she asked, her voice lilting at the end.

I shook my head. "No, definitely not. We have to go."

"We do?" She sounded surprised.

"Yes, we had this meeting, and then we need to go sign some paperwork for the marriage license."

Her eyes went wide. The sound of her swallowing was audible in the empty space. "Oh, right. That's one part of the wedding I haven't figured out. We have to decide who's going to marry us. Janet offered. She has her marriage commissioner appointment."

"Really?"

"She does," Phoebe replied with a smile.

"I'd love for Janet to marry us," I said, thinking that felt just right. I glanced at my watch. "We should go."

I opened the door, pausing to glance down. "Dinner tonight after that?"

Phoebe stared up at me before she nodded. Then she bit her lip, and I wanted to kiss her all over again. If there was a bed in this house, I didn't think we'd be leaving. Not if I had anything to say about it.

———

When we stopped by to pick up the marriage license, I could sense Phoebe's mounting anxiety about the situation. When we left, I looked over at her. "Let's go get dinner now."

Her eyes flicked to the dashboard. "It's only five."

"We've dealt with some big things, and you look stressed. There's no rule that we can't have dinner at five."

She narrowed her eyes. "I'm not stressed, Archer. It's just, well, *a lot*. Okay, maybe I am stressed." Her breath came out in a gust.

I smiled. "Yeah, let's have dinner."

"Do we have to go out?"

I shrugged. "We can do whatever you want."

"Why don't you come to my place? We can get takeout. We can do dinner out another time."

Chapter Ten

PHOEBE

I shouldn't have been so nervous, or that was what I kept telling myself. It was just Archer. There was nothing to be nervous about, but it didn't matter. I was still nervous. I needed to succumb to this and stop fighting it.

I'd gone a little bit crazy in my brain when he said he'd wanted to kiss me and when I'd admitted to him that I wanted to kiss him. Archie... I was kissing Archie.

He's not Archie anymore.

My cheeks got hot just thinking about it. Archer had dropped me off at the Willow Brook Fire & Rescue station, where I was going to pick up the jacket I'd left there. I also needed to let my superintendent know I was going to take the full two weeks off before the wedding and after. We hadn't even discussed a honeymoon.

"Oh, my god."

I didn't realize I'd spoken out loud when Paisley prompted, "Oh, my god, what?"

I whipped around to see her walking into the women's locker room at the fire station.

"Should I close the door?" Paisley asked, her eyes twinkling as she looked over at me.

My hand was curled on the edge of my locker, the cool steel doing nothing to chill the hot flashes running in cycles through my body. If I was older, I'd wonder if I was experiencing early menopause.

I must've stared too long because Paisley closed the door and asked, "What the hell is going on with you?"

I released my locker door and plunked down on the bench running the length of the room in front of the lockers. Paisley sat across from me on the opposite bench.

"I think I'm losing my mind," I said bluntly.

"Oh, really? I kind of already thought so," Paisley said lightly.

"Huh?"

"Girl, you've agreed to a marriage of convenience to save the environment. I mean, that is admirable, I suppose, but do you really need to get married for that?"

I rested my elbows on my knees, dropping my face into my palms. My breath filtered through my fingers as I let out a deep sigh. I tunneled my hands through my hair as I lifted my head and leaned my shoulders against the lockers.

"I don't think it's that crazy," I protested.

My friend eyed me skeptically. "It seems a little out of left field. That's all I'm saying," she finally said after a hesitation.

The locker room door opened, and Susannah, the third female firefighter in Willow Brook, entered. Madison was right behind her. While Paisley was wearing overalls and a T-shirt and Susannah was dressed in her fire gear, Madison looked straight out of a magazine. Her hair was twisted in some kind of knot I probably couldn't even do and her nails were bright purple and beautifully done.

Madison smiled amongst us, asking, "Is it okay that I come in? Graham is on the phone in his office."

Paisley patted the bench beside her. "Have a seat."

Susannah divided a look between us before sitting down beside me. "I don't know what it is, but it'll be fine," she offered.

"Is it Archer?" Madison asked.

She was more perceptive than she let on.

"Of course, it's Archer," Paisley replied. "I'm still trying to figure out why it's a good idea for her to get married to save the environment."

"They were best friends growing up. It's not like he's a stranger," Susannah offered loyally.

"He's definitely not a stranger," I affirmed.

"What's up?" Susannah asked. She slid an arm across my shoulder and squeezed before shifting back to lean against the lockers beside me.

"I kissed Archer," I said bluntly.

"Ooh, cups up," Madison said.

"What does that mean?" I asked.

"It's a spin-off from the whole spilled tea metaphor, that kind of thing. Archer is very hand-some. Not my type, but very handsome. I don't blame you for kissing him," Madison said.

"Not your type?" I asked.

She arched a brow. "Obviously not. Rugged fire-fighters are my type. Archer's a businessman, although he doesn't really look the part."

"He grew up in Alaska," I protested, feeling protective of him.

"I don't care what he is. He's completely hot," Paisley chimed in.

Susannah giggled at my side. She lifted her hands to tighten her ponytail. "He's definitely not Archie anymore."

"I know. I look at him, and I can't even think of how we used to be," I offered.

"Were you two really besties growing up?" Paisley asked.

"Absolutely. Our parents were friends, and we did everything together, all the way through middle school before he moved away."

"Then Tasha moved to town and became her best friend." Susannah rolled her eyes. "I saw her in town. She's worried about the wedding and really wants you to be in it."

"I know, but I'm not going to do that." I slid my eyes to hers and shrugged. "We saw her at Firehouse Café."

"Yeah, we heard about the hot kiss in the parking lot," Madison said, leaning forward as she lifted a finger in the air.

"Oh, god, who told you?" Heat flashed up my face.

"Janet," Paisley said.

"And Holly," Madison added.

"Oh." I sighed. "Tasha thinks I'm upset because of my ex, but I'd already broken up with him. It's her. I can't believe she did that."

"Yeah, because you're a really good friend. That's why Archer never forgot you and probably why he wants to marry you," Susannah said. "Plus, if that kiss was anything like I heard, this whole thing is *not* fake."

"I'm freaking out," I finally said. "He wants me to move in. He had an interior decorator out to his parents' place. He hired Amelia and Lucy to do some updates. I'm just..." I let out something between a groan and a growl. "I'm starting to think I'm crazy, but he asked because he needs to get married to take control of this part of the company. Why do rich people do weird shit like that?"

"Because rich people are weird," Madison chimed in. "For what it's worth, marriage is considered a stability factor and assessed as part of the risk in some business valuations." I started laughing. "I used to be rich. I know this shit. Trust me, being rich does not make them better people, although I'm sure Archer's parents are very nice. Is this their clause?"

I shook my head. "No, his grandmother's. If he doesn't get married, his great-uncle, his grandmother's brother-in-law, retains control."

"You don't have to go through with this if you're not ready," Susannah said quietly.

I glanced at her. "I know I don't, but I want to, and that's what's got me freaking out."

"We will all be there and support whatever you do," she added.

"I'm kind of excited about the wedding," Madison declared. "As big as his family's company is, Willow Brook will probably be in the news."

I rolled my eyes. Straightening, I took a deep breath. "I think I need to lay off kissing him. Then I can think more clearly."

"Sure, I'm sure you can do that," Madison said wryly, her lips twitching at the corners.

"I can," I insisted. "I didn't kiss him *ever* until now."

"Yeah, well, he hasn't been around for you to kiss him," Susannah pointed out.

Meanwhile, Paisley was biting her lip to keep from laughing.

I sighed. "Whatever."

"Are you on duty this week?" Paisley asked.

I shook my head. "Graham and I talked about me taking it off, but I came by to confirm with him. I'm going to take a month off. I have the leave, and it's our quiet season."

Madison nodded. "Well, I'm on top of the wedding planning, but have you decided who's going to officiate?"

"Janet. I confirmed it with Archer, and he's on board."

Madison smiled. "All right, girl, I'll keep planning. This is fun. I haven't gotten to use these skills in a while."

"What skills?" Paisley asked.

"My planning skills. I plan a good party," she said, waving her hand airily. "Do you need me to plan your wedding? I'll do it for free."

Paisley's cheeks flushed pink. "We're not even engaged yet."

Madison shrugged and winked at Susannah and me. "She will be soon. Take my word for it."

After talking to Graham, I was walking out the front a bit later when Maisie called my name. "What's up?" I stopped by the counter that encircled her desk.

"I heard about the kiss," she whisper-shouted.

Heat blasted my cheeks, and I pressed my lips together as I narrowed my eyes. "You're gossiping. How long have I known you?"

"As long as you've been back in town," she said with a shrug.

"Who did you hear about it from?" I couldn't help but ask. I was trying to suss out just how fast the kiss gossip was spreading.

"Mae Townsend was driving by and told me."

I groaned.

"Archer is..." She cleared her throat and waggled her eyebrows. "Handsome."

"Oh, yeah?"

"For sure," she teased. "Beck says he's a really nice guy."

"Yeah, Beck grew up with him."

"So did you. Isn't that your excuse for going through with this crazy marriage?" I rolled my eyes, and she continued, "Although, lots of people in town are happy about it."

"What do you mean?"

"Rumor has it, if Archer gets control of that company, people are hoping he's going to shut down the mine. The world's practically on fire these days. We could use a few glimmers of hope," she offered with a grin.

I laughed as I shook my head. "Do you think I'm crazy?"

"No crazier than me for marrying Beck," she replied matter-of-factly.

I burst out laughing. "Why do you say that? You have two kids, and you're still madly in love." It was downright endearing to see how Beck had grown into a committed, family guy.

"Well, he was a horrible flirt, but I went for it anyway. I don't think Archer's a flirt."

"No, he doesn't have that vibe," I commented.

"Beck is still a flirt, and I love it."

I walked out, thinking it must be nice to be that confident in someone's love. I was over my ex, but the hit to my trust lingered. That was a mark in Archer's favor because I trusted him completely.

ARCHER

I walked down the hallway at the place where Phoebe told me I could find her apartment. It was right next door to Firehouse Café. When I'd stopped by to grab a coffee earlier, Janet had told me she owned the building, and Phoebe rented one of two apartments upstairs. At that, she'd waggled her eyebrows and offered that the other apartment was empty.

"I'm getting the house updated as fast as I can, so we'll be able to stay there by the wedding."

"Phoebe's moving in with you?"

It was hard to surprise Janet, and I almost laughed when her brows rose to her hairline. "Yes, that's the plan. We *are* getting married after all."

A smile broke across her face at that, and she leaned over to squeeze my elbow. "I love that you two are getting married. It's perfect. I am worried, though," she added as she rang me up.

"Worried about what?"

"You haven't lived in Willow Brook in years. This is a small town. Are you planning to stay? What's going to happen with Phoebe and your work?"

These were all questions that had tumbled through my mind, but I'd been telling myself we'd sort it out, and it would all be okay. "Janet, my parents lived here for years. I grew up here. We can live here. I'm not planning to take Phoebe away."

"Well, we only just got her back about a year ago," Janet said as she eyed me skeptically.

"I know."

I felt that same sense of possessiveness I heard in Janet's voice. Phoebe was a treasure, and I knew that Janet knew it. I loved her all the more for that.

"We haven't hammered out all the details, but we'll work out where we're going to live, and we will definitely be in Willow Brook plenty."

"You've turned out to be a good man, Archer Cannon," Janet said when she handed me my change. When I dumped it into the tip jar, she rolled her eyes. "That change was more than your coffee." I shrugged. "You need to take her out to dinner in town."

"I suggested the same thing."

"There's a new pizza place and also, the gallery. I don't know if you've been there yet."

"I've seen it but haven't stopped in."

"Well, they have a little café now, and it's delicious. Every week is a different theme. You could find out what they have tonight and surprise Phoebe."

"Ah, she'd like that. She always was adventurous when it came to food."

Janet grinned, and I saw her look past my shoulder. I realized I was holding up the line.

"Sorry about that." I quickly stepped to the side as she handed me my coffee over the counter.

Hours later, I crested the top stair and looked down the hallway at Phoebe's building. My footsteps echoed on the hardwood floors. One door had a small welcome mat outside. I assumed that had to be Phoebe's if the other place was empty. As soon as I lifted my hand to rap my knuckles on the door, my heartbeat thudded faster. My reaction to Phoebe was startling in both its intensity and unexpectedness. When I'd thought about coming back and realized we could reconnect as friends, and then heard what her ex had done with her friend, it seemed like a mutually beneficial arrangement for us to get married. Marriage of convenience or not, I cared about her deeply. I simply hadn't expected to want her like this, emotionally and physically on a visceral level.

The door swung open while my hand was lifted.

"I was wondering when you were going to knock," Phoebe said, her eyes flicking to my hand as it dropped before shifting back to my face and then to the large paper bag I held in my other hand.

"What's that?"

"Dinner."

"You already got dinner? Is that leftovers?"

"Of course not. I didn't eat without you, Phoebe. I decided to surprise you. Janet suggested I pick up some takeout from the Gallery Café. This week's theme is Caribbean food."

Her eyes widened, and she clapped her hands. My heart flipped in my chest.

"I'm so excited! They just started doing that a couple of weeks ago, and I haven't tried it yet."

She waved me through the door, shutting it behind me. "Just hang your coat up here." She gestured to a row of hooks on the wall. On the floor below that was a tray for shoes.

"Should I take my shoes off?" My eyes shifted to her feet, which were encased in polka-dotted purple socks.

"Sure."

Those socks were *so* Phoebe. She loved bright colors when she was little, often wearing vibrant and whimsical clothes. It was funny to see the preference carry over into adulthood.

She took the bag from me. After I shrugged out of my jacket and shoes, I followed her over to an island that served as a natural divider between the efficiency kitchen and the open living space.

I glanced around, commenting, "This is nice."

When I met her eyes again, she rolled hers. "It's tiny. I'm sure wherever you live, you have a fancy-schmancy house or condo or apartment. I don't even know. Where *do* you live, Archer?"

"I live in Willow Brook now."

A wash of pink bloomed on her cheeks. She didn't reply and opened the bag to peer inside. "What do you mean?"

"I mean, I'm moving here. Have I not made that clear yet?"

Her doubtful eyes lifted to mine, and I could feel her searching as if she was trying to read into something I was hiding. I had nothing to hide. Well, except for the fact that I was afraid I was already falling in love with my old friend. This was so unexpected and unsettling.

"How long are you going to stay?" She lifted out one of the takeout containers and set it on the counter.

I reached for her hand as I slid my hips onto a stool. "Phoebe, come here," I added when she turned to face me. I reached for her other hand, and she stepped a little closer.

She stood between my knees, her worried and doubtful eyes searching mine. Emotion rose swiftly inside. I wanted her to understand, to trust I wouldn't hurt her.

"I reached out to you because I planned to come back. I know we kept in touch sporadically, but I always wished I'd done a better job."

The sound of her swallowing was audible. Then she licked her lips, and I wanted to kiss her. I shackled my need and curled my hands around hers. They were cool, and I sensed she was nervous. "I told you why I needed to get married, but if we're going to do this, I need to be here. And I want to be here. I really do."

She took a quick breath. "But don't you need to be there? Where do you live? I don't even know."

"Most recently, Seattle. You know our family's business started in Fireweed Harbor. We have offices in Seattle as well. I like the city, but I'm not deeply attached to it. Willow Brook has always been home to me because it's where I grew up. Sure, I'll need to travel for business, but with the internet these days, I don't need to be in one spot. I can work from here. On the occasions that I need to travel, I will. If you want, you can come with me. I know you like your job, but you don't have to work."

"I'm working," Phoebe interjected quickly.

She'd already made it clear she didn't feel comfortable about the financial imbalance between us. I wasn't sure how to reassure her that I didn't give a shit about that. Not even one bit.

She stared at me, catching and worrying her bottom lip with her teeth. The need to kiss her pressed inside, burning hot. Fierce need seemed to be a permanent state whenever I was near her. Not practical, but realistic nonetheless.

"Okay. Archer—" She began before stopping abruptly.

"What?" I prompted.

"This is feeling really *real*."

"It never was a joke," I said, trying to keep my tone light.

She started worrying her bottom lip again. Fuck me.

Leaning forward, I brushed a kiss over her mouth. She went still as I drew away, a deeper flush blooming across her cheeks and her eyes widening slightly.

"What was that for?" she whispered.

"I thought maybe you could stop chewing your lip," I teased.

"This is a bad idea."

"What?" I knew what she was asking, but for reasons I didn't understand entirely, I needed her to explain it.

"Getting married. And are we *really* getting married?"

"For the purposes of this, yes, we are."

She sucked in a quick breath. "I'm over my ex. I don't have to make a point to Tasha anymore."

"I know."

"But I do think it'd be awesome if you closed the mine," she added earnestly.

I laughed softly, and she started giggling. A moment later, we were both laughing so hard we were wiping tears from our faces. There was no one better to laugh with than Phoebe.

When we finally sobered, she brushed her tears away, and I dragged my sleeve across my face, taking a deep breath and letting it out in a gust. "I forgot how good it feels to laugh with you."

"I know." Her eyes were twinkling.

As we stood there staring at each other, it felt as if candles were being lit in the air around us, one after another, the flames racing into each other and creating heat and sparks that lifted and shimmered around us.

"It'll be okay," I said quietly.

"I know. I trust you," she whispered.

"Plus, I don't want to get married to anybody else."

"What do you mean?"

"Just that."

"I'd kind of sworn off relationships. They're too complicated, and I'm not a catch."

"What the hell do you mean?" I exclaimed.

Phoebe rolled her eyes. "I'm a hotshot firefighter, so most guys consider me a tomboy. They're either intimidated or want to be all tough and dominating and show me who the man is. It's just that after the whole thing happened with Tasha, well, trust is kind of hard to come by." Shadows chased through her eyes, and my heart twisted sharply. "But I trust you."

"Same."

Fuck, I wanted to kiss her again, but I held back. I was quickly discovering this was a balancing act. Faced with the unsettling intensity of my response to her, I also knew I needed to proceed with caution. I was relieved she at least admitted there was chemistry between us, but I didn't think she was ready for more.

Despite our friendship or perhaps because of our friendship.

"Our food's going to get cold if we don't eat soon," I commented, nudging my head in the direction of the takeout bag. I squeezed her hands, releasing them as she stepped back and rounded to the other side of the island.

"You get the rest of the food out, and I'll get the plates. What did you get anyway?" she asked, shifting into busy mode.

"It's kind of like a buffet setup, but not really. They

give you something of everything from whatever the weekly theme is when you're getting takeout. So, I'm not really sure what all we have."

"I love this! We should do this every week," she said with a lopsided grin in my direction.

Minutes later, Phoebe was sitting at an angle across from me at the island with her feet hooked around the rungs of a stool. She opened up the takeout containers, oohing and aahing over each option.

"Wow, this is really good," I said after I finished tasting the spicy tempura baked sweet potatoes.

"I know. I like the plan to rotate the themes, but they could do the Caribbean one every week," she replied between bites.

My heartbeat kicked harder as I looked over at her. I took a sip of water before my words slipped out unbidden. "It's really good to see you, Phoebe."

Her head whipped up, her hands stilling from where she had speared a piece of fish with her fork. "It's really good to see you, Archer."

"We sort of stayed in touch. I wish I'd been better about it."

"We were young, and social media wasn't that established yet. You're still my best friend," she said simply. Pink tinged her cheeks. "Tasha turned out not to be such a great next best friend in high school."

I shrugged. "I think she feels bad, for what it's worth."

Phoebe took a bite, chewing before replying, "I know she does."

"You're loyal, and you would never do that, even if you had been attracted to some guy she dated," I offered.

Phoebe took another bite, her lips pressing in a

line after she finished chewing. "Exactly. I'll get over it."

"I'd suggest we don't have to steal their thunder with our wedding, but the wheels are already in motion."

She shrugged. "It's okay. I'm actually kind of excited. Not because of the thunder stealing but because I think it'll be fun."

"Madison seems on top of the wedding planning," I teased.

"You can say that again. She's really into it." Phoebe grinned. "Thank God because wedding planning is definitely not in my wheelhouse."

"So, tell me, how'd you end up becoming a hotshot firefighter?" I was genuinely curious.

Between bites, she explained, "Well, I was in college, and you know I love the outdoors."

"Of course, same."

"I did some volunteer firefighter work in the city. It's different from hotshot work, but I loved it. I know I can't do this job long term, but I thought it'd be a good option for now."

"What's the plan after that?"

"I got my degree in wildlife biology, so I'll play it by ear."

"Our foundation raises money for wildlife conservation programs here in Alaska."

She finished chewing a bite and reached to take a swallow from her wine glass. Setting it down, she cocked her head to the side. "Archer, you don't have to support me, and you don't have to find work for me."

"I know, I know. I'm just saying. Plus, we don't even know where we might be in five years."

"We might not even still be married," she said with a shrug.

The urge to correct her on that detail was powerful, but I kept my mouth shut and made a noncommittal sound in my throat before taking a swallow from my beer.

"Your turn," she began next. "Obviously, I know you work for your family, and you're going to take over this entire branch of the business, but catch me up. What did I miss?"

"What do you mean?" I countered.

"Your whole life since high school. The last time we hung out was in middle school. Who was your first girlfriend? What was she like? How was college? So on and so forth." Phoebe circled her hand in the air.

I held her eyes, thinking I wished she'd been at my side all those years. Although, somehow, I didn't think we would have ended up here if that had been the case. Maybe this was better. I quickly sketched the outlines of my life for her. There was one area I tended to always gloss over because it hurt. The details related to it were a part of why I was sitting here.

If I could tell anyone, it was Phoebe. I took a breath, steeling myself for the self-inflicted blow because talking about this was like dragging a jagged blade across my heart and tearing off an old scab. "You remember my cousin Jake?"

Phoebe nodded immediately. "Yeah, you too were pretty close, right?"

"He died."

She gasped, her palm flying to her chest. "Oh, no. Archer, what happened?"

Reaching over, she placed her hand on my knee. Her touch was soothing but also distracting. "It's part of the reason my great-uncle hates me. We went to college together. He died of alcohol poisoning at a party. I'd left early because I never was much of a partier. He drank himself into a stupor and died. Clint said I should have been there. I think he knows, obviously, I couldn't be my cousin's keeper, but it led to some bad blood between us. He's always resented me for being alive while his grandson was dead." I was leaving out some major details that played into the entire mess and the likely reason my cousin had become a young alcoholic, but I could only handle so much. Some secrets were meant to be taken to the grave, or so I'd convinced myself over the years.

"He's furious about the clause for me to take over the company once I'm married. He currently manages this branch of the business and can't do anything about it if I get married."

I took a breath, loosening the tension banded around my chest.

"I'm really sorry about Jake. I know you were close." The warmth in her eyes soothed the sting from that scab being torn off.

"Thank you. It's life, and shit happens, or something like that." That was a massive understatement, but even telling her this pushed me to the edge inside.

I managed to move our conversation onto lighter topics, regaling her with a few stories about my grandmother. Phoebe actually knew her because she'd come to visit a few times when we were little. Though my grandmother was mostly wheelchair bound now, she still had all of her faculties and wielded her power strategically.

Chapter Twelve

PHOEBE

Being with Archer was discombobulating. On the one hand, it was completely comfortable and familiar. Even though we hadn't seen each other since fifth grade, I still *knew* him and our old friendship felt like pulling on a comfy sweater. On the other, it was disconcerting to be so attracted to him. I'd catch myself letting my eyes linger on him. He was easy on the eyes with his dark blond hair, that shade of stubble, and his smoky-gray gaze.

The features that had seemed almost square and blocky when he was little were now chiseled. I knew he was the kind of man women crushed on. I wasn't one to crush on any man. Yet here I was, crushing *hard* on him. I wasn't much for dating. Trying to date in my old hometown had felt impossible. There weren't many options, at least not for me.

After we cleaned up from dinner, we lingered at the counter.

"How tall are you?" I asked when he angled on his stool to face me. It seemed like his knees were practically folding into themselves.

A laugh rustled in his throat, and my belly swooped. "Six-two. I'm definitely taller than I was in middle school."

"Well, yeah."

"How tall are you?"

"Not that much taller than I was in middle school," I deadpanned.

He threw his head back with a laugh. This time, my belly did a shimmy and a swoop.

"I think I've grown maybe three inches since middle school. If I stand up really straight, I can say I'm five-four."

He smiled at me, and I felt caught in the beam of his gaze.

"It's really good to see you, Phoebe," he said.

"You said that before."

"Well, it bears repeating." He rested an elbow on the counter, and my toes curled more tightly on the rung of my stool. "I didn't know what it'd be like to see you again."

"I didn't either, and it had been a while. How many years was it?"

"We're both thirty, so…"

"We haven't seen each other since we were eleven," I finished. "People change a lot from middle school."

"Do they, though? Coming back here, I've run into a lot of people I knew back then. Maybe they're a little different, but the underlying part is the same."

"What do you mean?"

"Well, take Beck. He's totally a flirt and a tease, but he was a loyal guy before. It doesn't surprise me that he's happily married and already has two kids. He was that kind of friend."

I cocked my head to the side. "I suppose you're right."

"And Cade, he was kind of serious back then, and he's kind of serious now. He's got a sense of humor, but you know what I mean."

"True."

"And you, you were a tomboy then. It suits you perfectly that you're a hotshot firefighter now."

"Am I still a tomboy?" I heard myself asking but then immediately chastised myself. *Don't ask stupid, leading questions.*

"I don't know if tomboy is the word now, but you were tough. You weren't a girly girl then, and you're not now. It doesn't change the fact that you're beautiful and totally sexy."

"What?" I squeaked.

"I said what I said," Archer replied, his lips kicking up in a teasing smile. "What about me?"

"What do you mean, what about you?"

"Am I like I was in fifth grade?" he asked.

I caught my bottom lip in my teeth as I pondered his question. The answer came quickly. "Mostly, but not completely."

"How?"

"Well, I don't think of you as Archie anymore, which is kind of funny. But that doesn't really matter." I gestured vaguely in the air. "You're just solid and stable. And good. You're still funny, but you're not goofy. I'm not sure if you're different or if it's me, but—"

His eyes met mine, searching. "What do you mean?"

"You run a billionaire company now, or part of one," I clarified, feeling flustered.

"Yeah, so did my parents before," he said, all nonchalant.

"I didn't think of you like that, though," I pressed.

"Because my parents weren't snobs who flashed their money. I'm not either. I think that's your idea about me."

"Maybe so," I said cautiously.

"Money doesn't define a person unless you let it."

Archer rested his hand across the back of my stool. Even though he wasn't even touching me, I could feel the heat radiating from his hand where it rested just behind my shoulders.

"I feel like I don't have the best judgment about people," I offered.

"Because of Tasha?"

I nodded. "It really shocked me when I learned she screwed around with my boyfriend behind my back. I just didn't think she would do that. I didn't think she was that kind of person."

"Good people can do shitty things, and bad people can do good things." Archer was philosophical, and I supposed it was true.

"What's the worst thing you've done?"

Archer tilted his head to the side, his fingertips drumming behind my shoulders. A prickle chased down my spine.

"You and I did some pretty crazy stuff when we were little. In high school, I got in trouble for drag racing after I got my license."

"What?!" I gasped.

He threw me a lopsided grin. "I know. It was totally fucking stupid. There's a reason insurance rates are much higher for guys up until they're twenty-five. We're stupid."

"What happened?"

"It was a dare with some friends. I got caught, and my parents actually pulled my license."

"What do you mean?"

"In most states, your parents have to consent to you having your license. It took me six months to earn it back. I never did that again. Hell, I was afraid to speed after that."

"Do you speed now? Because I'm usually driving at least five miles an hour over the limit," I offered.

Archer rolled his eyes. "Maybe about that much, but that's it." I giggled. "And what's the craziest thing you did?" he asked.

I shrugged. "I don't know. I guess fighting fires is pretty crazy."

"Is it?" Archer pressed.

"I mean, it's definitely risky. There's an adrenaline rush to the job, and we jump out of helicopters and airplanes into the wilderness."

"I bet you're good at it," he said confidently.

"Why do you say that?"

I really wanted to know his answer. Not to stroke my ego but I was curious to understand how he saw me.

"Because you were always a bit of a daredevil when we were kids. Whenever we did something crazy, you did it first. Like the cliff diving at that river."

I laughed, recalling the river where we'd gone to a few times to dive in from the rocky ledge above. "Oh, yeah? You called me the test case."

"Exactly. You've got nerve. I can't imagine you getting rattled about much of anything. Do you like your crew?"

"I do. It's a solid group. It's nice not to be the only woman at the station."

"How many women are hotshots?"

"Three, including me. You met Paisley, and you probably remember Susannah Gilmore." At his nod, I continued, "She's on the town crew, and she's married to Ward, who's a superintendent for another crew."

"I bet you intimidate the guys on your crew," Archer said with a dip of his chin. He lifted his beer to take a swallow, and my eyes snagged on the motion of his throat.

Gah! I could go gaga over this guy's throat. Jesus, I needed to get a grip.

"Phoebe?" he prompted.

Whipping my eyes up to his, I hoped he couldn't tell I was salivating over his throat. I could smell him from here. We were only sitting a foot or so apart, and he had this kind of clean, crisp, ocean-y sent to him. I scrambled to try to remember what he had said. "Oh, you think? I don't think they're intimidated by me."

"I do," he argued.

I shrugged. "Actually, Russell used to be intimidated by Paisley."

"I haven't connected all the dots, but aren't Russell and Paisley together?" I nodded. "So why was Russell intimidated by her?"

"Because he had a crush on her, which is exactly why none of the guys are intimidated by me."

Archer gave me a long look, his eyes darkening to charcoal. I swallowed, trying to ignore the heat spinning through me.

"I like my job, but I definitely won't be there forever. Physically, it's hard. The pay is decent but not amazing."

He nodded. I could tell he wanted to say something about money, so I couldn't help but prompt, "Go ahead. Say it."

"Say what?" He took another swallow of his beer, distracting me again with his throat.

When he set the bottle down, I lifted my chin and

narrowed my eyes. "You know what. You wanted to remind me again that I don't need to worry about money."

"Well, you don't, Phoebe. You're doing me a big favor."

I opened my mouth to say he was doing the same for me, but I held back. Initially, I'd been feeling petty, and I'd wanted to get back at my friend. Even though I was over my ex, I didn't mind making him squirm. But I didn't have that feeling anymore.

I shrugged lightly, not about to divulge any of my emotional confusion to Archer. "Hey, it's all about saving the environment. You know how they talk about ripples and things?" He nodded. "It'll be a good ripple in the world to close that mine for good."

His chuckle was low and husky and made my insides feel funny.

"We'll save a few salmon runs while we're at it," I offered.

This time, he threw his head back with a deep laugh. "I'm all about making sure the salmon can spawn. Maybe we should have a salmon-themed wedding?"

I burst out laughing, and he laughed along with me. By the time we sputtered out, we were both gasping for air and swiping tears from our eyes. There was nothing like a good belly laugh, and I'd forgotten how often I shared those with Archer. You tend to laugh more like that when you're young, but we'd also had that kind of friendship. Apparently, we still did.

As we stared at each other, something shimmered to life between us. Perhaps it had been there all along. Certainly, the attraction, but this wasn't any old attraction. It was fiery hot, sparking like electricity and heating the space around us. I could hear the rush of blood in my ears. My entire body was combusting, and I couldn't think. Of all the men I'd have guessed could make me forget myself, I would never have thought it could be Archer. *Never*.

Gulping in air, I knew my cheeks were flushed because I was hot all over. I lifted my wine glass, rolling it between my palms. For the life of me, I couldn't look away from his gaze. Thank god I wasn't standing. I was certain my knees would've given way, and he would've had to catch me to keep me from falling.

I cleared my throat and meant to say something. Anything sensible would've done the trick. Instead, I whispered, "Archer." Even to my ears, it sounded like a plea.

He gave my hand a little tug. "Come here, Phoebe."

I was practically hypnotized as I slipped my hips off the stool. On wobbly knees, I took two steps until I stood between his.

He lifted a hand, his fingers sliding through the ends of my hair just over my shoulder. I felt his knuckles brushing along my collarbone and underneath my jaw. My pulse was racing so fast, I almost felt as if I couldn't be contained in my own body. Sensations zinged around inside, colliding and creating more and more heat and electricity.

Apparently, all I could say was his name. "Archer," I whispered again.

I watched as he lowered his head, his silver-smoke gaze on mine. I let out something like a whimper the second his lips brushed over mine. I swear, sparks flew in the air between us.

I whispered his name into his mouth. Our kiss went from that subtle, almost testing point of contact to hot, deep, and wild. His hand slid to cup my nape, and I moaned shamelessly. He adjusted the angle of my head and fit his mouth over mine, taking full command of our kiss.

I didn't know if what I was doing was considered surrender, but that's what it felt like. I simply surrendered to the sensations, to the need, to the pure, fierce *want* roaring inside me. It felt as if a dam had broken loose. My need was a river, rushing and sweeping me in its current, and my only choice was to let it carry me away. Anything else was impossible.

Chapter Thirteen

ARCHER

Phoebe moaned into our kiss. Every sound she made sent a sizzle of lightning through my body. Holy hell. She tasted so good—sweet with hints of plummy wine on her tongue.

This being our third kiss, I discovered something about her. Each one started with her slightly tense. Then the second she let go, it felt as if something snapped loose inside her. She threw herself into kisses with abandon once that happened. The stiffness eased from her as her body softened against mine. With one hand half-tangled in her hair, I slid my other down her back, gliding over the sweet dip of her waist and the lush curve of her bottom.

Satisfaction sizzled through me when she let out another moan as I rocked my arousal into the cradle of her hips as I drew her closer to me. I was hard. Fuck, *so* hard. She probably felt like she was being prodded by a hot tire iron.

This wasn't supposed to be complicated. It was, and it wasn't. If I didn't let my thoughts get in the way, nothing was difficult with Phoebe. Everything felt good with her, including losing myself in the warm sweetness of her mouth, savoring the way her tongue teased against mine. The feel of her hand slipping under my shirt was cool against my warm skin. I meant to control this encounter, to keep it from spiraling out of my reach, but that was nearly impossible.

We were here alone with no convenient interruptions. One kiss tumbled into the next, and I breathed her in, absorbing the imprint of her curves against my body. I slid my palm up, letting it slip under the hem of her shirt. Her skin was silky soft, and she trembled slightly when I broke free from her mouth. Pressing hot, open kisses along her jaw and neck, I savored the feel of goose bumps rising on her skin.

"Archer!" She gasped when I let my palm graze over her breast.

Her nipple was a tight bead under the silk of her bra. "Hmm?" I murmured against her throat, just over the wild beat of her pulse.

Her reply was a whimper, followed by a moan. She arched her back, pressing into my touch. I cupped her breast fully. The weight of it was heavy and fit perfectly in my palm. I was feeling greedy and nipped her neck when I flicked the clasp loose between her breasts.

She breathed, "Yes, yes," when I rolled her nipple between my thumb and forefinger.

It wasn't enough. I leaned back, just enough to tug her shirt up. She gave me an assist, reaching for the collar and bringing it up over her head in an arching swoop to one side, where it tumbled to the floor in a rush of air.

We stared at each other for a moment, and I simply absorbed her. Her honeyed locks were in a messy tousle around her shoulders. Her skin was flushed everywhere, a pretty pink. Her lips were kiss-bitten, and her eyes were deep pools of blue. Her breath came in sharp little pants, and her breasts rose and fell with each gasp.

"You're beautiful," I rasped, meaning it in more ways than one.

Objectively speaking, she was beautiful. To me, she was fucking stunning. If I'd been standing, I would've fallen to my knees in worship. But it wasn't just that. It was Phoebe. My friend, the girl I knew so well. Certain friends came along in life where the connection was just easy. You knew each other in a way that others didn't, and the trust ran like a river, so deep that the supply was endless.

And now, to have all of that and have this blazing-hot chemistry striking lightning bolts into the air around us, everything became extra.

Her lips parted on a breath, and I dipped my head again because I had to taste her. I leaned down and captured one of her dusky pink nipples with my mouth. She cried out, her fingers spearing in my hair as I swirled my tongue around it. My teeth grazed over it with a light nip before I lifted my head. I transferred my attention to her other nipple. "Wouldn't want to leave anything out," I murmured when I lifted my head again.

Her lips were parted for a beat, and then we were kissing again, and I lost myself in her mouth as I took deep sips. I couldn't get enough. Mapping her with my hands, I learned every inch of her and savored the way she flexed under my touch. I quickly discovered she was sensitive just above her collarbone and shivered all over every time I touched her there.

I finally couldn't hold back anymore and let my

palm coast down over the sweet curve of her belly, unbuttoning her jeans swiftly and sliding my hand inside to find her silk panties drenched. She let out an inarticulate sound in her throat, her hips rocking into my touch.

Then it became messy and fumbling with very little finesse. I needed to feel her. I hooked my fingers under the edge of her panties to caress her silky folds, her arousal slicking my fingers. I dipped into her core, finding her clit swollen and needy.

I watched through heavy lids as her hips bucked against me. Her orgasm came fast, her pussy clenching around my fingers. I pressed over her clit and watched when her eyes flew open, and her whole body shuddered as she cried my name sharply.

I kept one arm wrapped tightly around her waist as the trembling slowed, pressing kisses on her neck.

Chapter Fourteen

PHOEBE

I was nearly melted against Archer and dragged my eyes open when I felt his touch withdraw. His eyes were on me as he lifted his fingers and licked them. Right in front of me! If he hadn't been holding me, I would've collapsed.

Another aftershock rippled through me when he did that. I had no idea how long we stood there as pleasure reverberated through my body. I felt profoundly sated on a bone-deep level I'd never experienced. Adrenaline was racing through my body in circles. I saw the same sense of wonderment and near shock in Archer's eyes.

"You're cold," he murmured.

His hands curved over my shoulders and down my arms, and I felt the goose bumps under his touch. I was shirtless with my jeans unbuttoned and shoved halfway down my hips. I felt in utter disarray.

Archer was still fully clothed. I was abruptly bashful, leaning over to scoop my shirt off the floor. When I straightened, he caught me by the shoulders again. "Hey," he said softly.

My cheeks were hot and not just from desire.

"You don't need to panic."

"I'm not panicking," I lied.

"I might be," he said flatly.

A hysterical laugh bubbled out of my throat as his arms slid around my waist. I let my forehead fall to his chest and took several deep breaths, trying to marshal my composure.

This was Archer, and just as I knew him well, he knew me so very well. There was no sense in trying to hide. Lifting my head, I brushed my hair off my shoulders as I clutched my shirt with my other hand.

"I don't know how to play this cool," I whispered.

"I don't either. So maybe we don't try. That's not what we're about anyway." His lips curled in a slow smile, and my heart flipped in my chest as butterflies spun in my belly.

A few minutes later, I had my shirt on and my jeans buttoned. I still couldn't play it cool, but at least I was dressed and felt a little more like myself. To be clear, it wasn't as if I hadn't felt like myself with Archer, but rather a wild, wanton, out-of-control version of myself.

"So where are you staying?" I asked. "Are you at your house yet?"

He shook his head. "Not yet."

"Where have you been staying?" I prompted.

"A hotel in Anchorage. Janet offered me the place across the hall from you, but she said it wasn't furnished because she was redoing it."

"You can stay here." I heard myself offering before I could think better of it.

What the hell are you thinking? I immediately chastised myself.

"Are you sure?" he asked.

Heat flared hot and fast in my cheeks, but I

managed to nod. "It seems silly for you to drive all the way to Anchorage every night and come back. Do you know when the furnishing situation will be dealt with at your house?"

"Sometime next week."

"Oh."

"Oh," Archer repeated, his eyes glinting with a slight smile. "Good timing, I figure. We can move in once they take care of a few basics."

I took a shuddering breath, and his hand reached across the counter to curl over mine where it rested. The moment he touched me, I felt both soothed and lit by a fire.

"Don't panic," he repeated.

I let out a shaky laugh. "It seemed so easy before you kissed me. Maybe it's more than we thought."

"And maybe that's a good thing."

When my eyes widened, he repeated, "Don't panic."

"Is your stuff at the hotel in Anchorage?" If I focused on the practical, maybe I could get a grip inside.

He shook his head. "I just keep it in my car. Between the work Amelia and Lucy are doing to get the bedroom, bathroom, and kitchen being updated and the furniture people bringing things in, I'm checking in every day. So, I'm never sure if I'll be there or here."

"Here?" My voice squeaked.

"Not here at your apartment, but here in Willow Brook. I wasn't banking on you inviting me to stay with you."

My heart got the best of me, its loud demand rising above the din of anxiety and uncertainty clamoring in my mind. "Just stay here." A nervous giggle escaped.

Archer's gaze darkened. "Can we make a deal?" he asked.

"Um, sure?"

"Let's save sex for our wedding night."

My mouth fell open as I stared at him. "Seriously? It's not like I'm a virgin, Archer. And I'm pretty sure you're not either."

He shook his head slowly, his lips quirking at the corners. "No, but I don't know. It's a way to keep something special."

"Do you think we can live together without that happening?" Since I'd already lost myself with him, I figured I might as well be blunt.

He shrugged. "Maybe. It's taking all I have not to pick you up and carry you into your bedroom right now to finish what we started."

My breath drew in sharply, and my heart lunged like the patter of hooves on hard ground, striking sparks.

"This week will give us time to get used to each other. It'll make it seem more real," I managed to say.

"It *is* real, Phoebe."

After that, Archer helped me tidy the kitchen.

"What do you usually do at night?" he asked when we settled into the couch in the living room.

I smiled sheepishly. "Watch TV until I get sleepy. Sometimes I read."

"You always did love to read."

"I still do."

"What do you read now?"

"Just about everything. Romance, mysteries, literature, sometimes nonfiction."

"The whole gamut," he murmured. His smile was warm. "What do you like to watch on TV?"

"Let's pick a show. Something relaxing," I insisted. "*Parks and Rec?* I love that show."

So that was how I found myself with my legs thrown over Archer's lap and his palm curled around my ankle. Somehow, I relaxed. I fell asleep later with him curled up beside me, his palm warm on my belly and the sound of his breath lulling me to sleep. I almost couldn't believe we were there.

Chapter Fifteen

ARCHER

The following morning, I came awake with a jolt. I cataloged my surroundings, my attention centering on Phoebe. I was lying on my back, and she was curled up against my side with her head tucked into my shoulder. I could feel the soft gusts of her breath against my skin. Her knee was hooked over my leg, inches away from my morning arousal. Her hand was resting on my abdomen, and she was sound asleep.

My arm was curled around her back, and I was copping a feel in my sleep because I had a nice handful of the lush curve of her bottom. I smiled to myself because I could get used to this.

My mind replayed last night, slides of the evening skipping from one moment to the next—when we had dinner, when I kissed her, when she came all over my fingers, then later relaxing on the couch, thinking how good it was to have my best friend back in vivid color.

Phoebe mumbled something, shifting against me and then falling back to sleep. I wanted to wake her up by rolling her over, planting a kiss on her, and mapping every inch of her body before burying myself inside her, but I didn't.

I sensed she wasn't ready for that. I was caught up in my own uncertainty. We had already crossed boundaries I hadn't even known existed until we came up to them and flew past the guardrails.

I wanted to fall back asleep, but I knew it was a lost cause. The sun hadn't even crested the horizon yet. Just when I thought I'd have to find a way to gracefully slip out of bed, Phoebe moved again, then mumbled, "You're awake."

I rolled my head to the side to find her lashes lifting. The light was dim in her bedroom. There was a night-light near the bed, casting just enough light I could see her eyes.

"So are you," I observed.

My heart was kicking forcefully against my ribs. I couldn't resist sliding my hand up her back, savoring the silky-smooth feel of her skin. I brushed her hair away from her face and dipped my head to give her a kiss. I meant for it to be brief, but as I was coming to learn, any kiss with Phoebe took on a life of its own.

Before I knew it, I was lingering, coaxing her lips open, tightening my fingers in her hair, and then laying a proper devouring kiss on her. She broke free with a gasp, followed by a startled laugh before she fell quiet.

"Archer?"

"Yes?"

She sighed. "I don't even know what to think."

"I think we should have coffee," I said.

I knew if I stayed in this bed with her, I'd lose my mind and any discipline I had. Oh, I wasn't going to just stick to kisses for the time until our wedding, but I couldn't be copping a feel every second I had with her.

"Coffee is perfect," she replied.

She rolled away, and I slipped out of bed quickly. Once I was standing, I asked, "Mind if I shower?"

"Of course not. You shower first. I'll start the coffee, then I'll shower."

She narrowed her eyes when she looked my way. "We're not showering together yet."

I chuckled. "Okay, we'll save that for later."

Moments later, I brought myself to a quick release in the shower and soaped off, telling myself that would tide me over until later. I had plans for Phoebe tonight, and they involved more than tasting her on my fingers.

When I walked down to the kitchen, she was wearing a robe. When she turned around, she looked so delectably adorable, I couldn't help but cross the kitchen and rest my hands on either side of her hips on the counter.

"You're beautiful in the morning," I murmured as I dipped my head and laid another kiss on her.

She looked flustered when I lifted my head. "You need to put a shirt on," she ordered.

"Okay," I said slowly, following her into the bedroom.

She stopped in the doorway to the bathroom. "By the time I come out, you'd better have a shirt on."

"Yes, ma'am," I teased.

She closed the door, and I pulled on a T-shirt. I returned to the kitchen, smiling when I discovered she'd left a mug by the coffee maker and a container of half and half. After I poured my coffee and took a few swallows, my phone rang. When I glanced down and saw it was from my office, I answered.

I discovered my mistake seconds later. "What the hell, Archer?" my great-uncle demanded. He didn't even bother with a hello, but then he was a genuine asshole.

"Excuse me?"

"Since when are you getting married?"

"Soon."

"This is bullshit."

"It's not bullshit," I said, trying to keep my cool. It wasn't bullshit, and I was pretty confident I was already in love with Phoebe. My only problem now was keeping her married to me.

A more pressing problem at this moment was my uncle's voice. My chest got tight, and my breathing felt constricted.

"How long have you known this woman?" Clint demanded.

"Since I was about two," I said.

"What the fuck?"

My heart started pounding in a familiar hard, sick beat that I hated. My breath felt short, and everything inside felt as if it was rushing. I tried to keep my vision focused on something, anything. I stared at my coffee mug, keeping my hand clenched around the handle. I felt sick as if I was falling.

"Archer!" he demanded.

Through the staticky cacophony in my brain, I felt Phoebe's palm on my back. Her touch was an anchor in the commotion outside of me. I blinked and heard myself saying, "I have to go."

I managed to lower the phone and drag my thumb across the screen, staring at it to confirm the call officially ended. Sometimes technology was a bitch, and the convenience of things staying open and live and logged on could be a fucking nightmare.

"Are you okay?" I heard Phoebe asking as I dragged in a quick breath.

She couldn't see my face because my back was to her. I held on to my composure or, rather, scrambled for it. I felt as if I was hanging on to the edge of a cliff. I needed to get a better grip and pull myself up.

The spots faded along the edges of my vision. The strange staticky, rushing feeling started to slow inside. I took a swallow of my coffee and finally felt composed enough to turn around. Her hand was still on my back, her touch sliding to my shoulder. I was relieved by that contact. The feel of it broke through the muddled sensations inside.

"I'm fine," I said, my voice sounding a little raspy. I took another quick swallow of coffee to mask it.

Her eyes skated over my face, her gaze probing and concerned. "Are you sure? That didn't sound like a pleasant phone call."

"It wasn't, but it's okay. It was just my great-uncle calling to yell at me because he found out I'm getting married."

"Which uncle is this again?"

"Clint, my grandmother's brother-in-law. The one who doesn't want me to have control of this company because he's a fucking asshole," I said bluntly. "She and my grandfather started the business, and Clint's always wanted to have a controlling stake, but he doesn't." I hated what he did and the effect he had on me. And I hated that Phoebe saw me like this.

I dragged in another breath and took another swallow of coffee. The sense of panic had receded, leaving me profoundly relieved.

I'd told Phoebe the truth about why I needed to get married originally. But there was an underlying truth that I hadn't told her or anyone other than one therapist. My parents didn't even know. They just knew I couldn't stand Clint. They didn't really like him either, so it was okay. We rarely saw him. When I started working in Seattle, I made efforts to avoid interacting with him and was relieved that he rarely came to the office, often working from home and relying on his assistant to keep him up to speed.

I set my phone down and lifted my free hand, resting it over hers on my shoulder and savoring her touch. She blinked, and our fingers tangled.

As I stared into Phoebe's eyes, that fuzzy whirling sensation—that was honestly terrifying and that I kept locked inside privately—faded completely.

The level of trust I had with Phoebe was something I didn't have with many people, probably no one other than my parents. Even they didn't know I experienced these fucking panic attacks. I'd thought I was having a heart attack the first time. My doctor had ruled out every heart problem under the sun and diagnosed me with a panic disorder. He'd suggested I talk to a therapist, and I'd reluctantly agreed.

I didn't like admitting weakness. I also didn't like being *that* kind of an asshole. I didn't want to think of myself as the kind of guy who couldn't acknowledge some feelings. But panic was so disconcerting, so utterly terrifying and inexplicable that it wasn't easy to explain. It was fucking hell to live through.

I felt safe with Phoebe. Even if I wasn't ready to tell her about this, I knew she wouldn't judge me. After several more beats of my heart, I started to relax. Often the panic receded quickly once its vise was released. It was like something snapped loose, followed by the reverberation of breaking free.

"Are you okay?" she asked quietly.

"Yeah."

Her eyes searched mine for another moment

before she leaned and pressed a kiss on my cheek. I moved on instinct, turning my face and catching her lips with mine.

In a blink, the kiss went from chaste to hot. Phoebe drew back with a husky laugh.

"Well, good morning to you."

"Sorry, not sorry," I said lightly. "You probably want some coffee. You did make it after all."

Her lips curled in a soft smile. She held onto my hand with her fingers laced loosely with mine while she poured a cup of coffee with the other.

"What do you like to have for breakfast?" she asked.

I nudged my chin toward the stools by the counter. Her knees bumped mine when we sat down beside each other.

"Okay, back to my question. What do you usually do for breakfast?"

"I'm a workaholic, Phoebe."

She peered up at me. "I suppose you probably are. I am too."

"I can be really bad about it," I added.

"How bad?" She rested an elbow on the counter and traced her fingertips along the edge.

"I don't think much about breakfast. I wake up, roll out of bed, and get coffee on the way to work. My assistant usually orders me something, a bagel probably."

"Oh, you have your own assistant?" Her eyes brightened.

"I do."

She sighed. "I keep forgetting you're really rich."

"My assistant is Brandon, and I trust him with my life." Brandon was the only person other than my doctor and therapist who knew about my panic attacks. He'd come into my office when I was in the midst of one.

These thoughts passed through my mind as Phoebe cocked her head to the side.

"The money part is weird for me," she announced.

"Oh? I hadn't noticed," I teased lightly.

She pressed her lips together, a little puff of air escaping when she released them. Warmth cinched around my heart. She'd done that ever since she was a little girl.

"You still do that," I observed.

"Still do what?"

I repeated the motion for her, adding a little exaggeration so it was obvious when I let my breath out.

"I do not!" she squeaked.

"You totally do. I love it."

She nudged my foot with hers. That subtle touch, playful and light, sent a sizzle through me. "Okay, back to breakfast. You liked bagels when we were kids."

"I still like bagels."

"Good. Should we go get some? Firehouse Café is right next door, so it's convenient."

I was actually enjoying being alone with Phoebe, but I was hungry.

"People will see us," she added.

"You know it's not just about that anymore, right?"

She looked confused. I reached for her hand, sliding my thumb in a slow pass across the inside of her wrist. A pretty flush bloomed on her cheeks. "I'm not faking. Maybe our reasons for starting this weren't genuine, but my feelings are."

I could tell she didn't know what to do with that because she started blinking rapidly.

"Don't think too hard, and please don't worry," I added. I leaned forward and pressed a quick and fierce kiss on her lips. When I drew back, she licked her lips, and I wanted to kiss her all over again. But if I did that, we'd never get out of here.

Twenty years ago

"Jake!" I called, smiling when I heard him laugh in reply.

I jogged around the back of the house to find my cousin running across the lawn ahead of me. We were at his family's vacation home on the coast of Washington. I loved coming here in the summers with my parents.

Jake tossed me the volleyball just before we got to the water. We passed the ball back and forth along the edge of the waves. We were exhausted a while later and decided to go back inside. On the way up, we stumbled across a yellow jacket hive in the ground. In a matter of seconds, we were swarmed with yellow jackets, both of us hollering and swatting at them as we rushed away.

We learned Jake was allergic to yellow jackets that day, and I watched as his mother hustled him into the car, calling over to me, "I called your mother. She'll be back soon."

After she drove away, I held up my arm, inspecting the stings on my forearm. Apparently, you could die from getting *stung by yellow jackets if you were allergic. I felt a little scared for Jake. The house was quiet once the sound of the door closing echoed behind me. The hardwood floor was cool under my bare feet as I walked down the hallway toward the kitchen.*

I didn't know anyone was home until I abruptly sensed motion behind me, just after I passed the doorway into the den. It was my great-uncle Clint. His eyes were red, and his face kind of blotchy, like it always was. "You're an idiot," he muttered.

I couldn't explain why, but I'd felt uneasy and on edge around him for the past year or so. Not that I'd ever felt comfortable around him, but lately, my instincts raised a red flag when he was near. Fortunately, he generally ignored me, along with my cousins. He didn't really seem to like kids.

When he stepped into the hallway, I nearly jumped but forced my feet to stay flat on the ground and stared at him. Before I could comprehend what was happening, he lifted his hand and slapped me across the face, so hard my head snapped back. I cried out, the sound ricocheting around the hallway.

"Wh-what?" I stuttered.

The next thing I knew, he had grabbed my arm and dragged me to the side of the hallway, where he drove his fists into my side. The pain was sharp and literally robbed my breath. I leaned against the wall, gasping as he stood over me. "Stay out of my way, and don't ever tell anyone what you saw."

He walked back into the den, closing the door quietly. The dots around the edges of my vision cleared. I was almost afraid to move, but I finally did. I tiptoed down the hallway and up the stairs into the room I shared with my cousin. I locked the door. There was a small latch, and it looked as awfully insubstantial as I felt. I didn't even know what my uncle was talking about, and I didn't want to know.

. . .

Present day

"Granddad thinks you're getting married to get control from him," Rhys said, his tone dry.

I adjusted the phone against my ear, replying to my cousin, "I'm not." The funny thing was that I had been originally. "I'm marrying Phoebe. She was my best friend when we were kids. You remember her?"

"I think so. She had blond hair, usually in ponytails or braids?" he replied.

"That's the one."

It felt as if my heart itself was smiling at that recollection. Memories of Phoebe were like sunshine falling in shafts through my life, illuminating the dark, cold spaces in my heart.

Rhys continued, "That's what I told him. I thought it was her. He's an ass. That's the reason your grandparents didn't give him full control of anything. He said he resents being a placeholder."

"Whatever," I muttered. "He should be pissed off at you."

Rhys Cannon, my cousin, and I shared duties in managing our family's business. We'd been close forever. The only secret I'd ever kept from him, aside from my panic attacks, was his grandfather and what he'd done. Rhys knew some of what Clint was capable of, but some secrets were best kept unsaid. No sense in allowing words to give them any more power. Although, I occasionally wondered if keeping that secret gave my great-uncle more power.

I simply wasn't prepared for the mess of speaking aloud about what he'd done. Rhys was oblivious to my wandering train of thought. "Maybe he should be pissed at me, but you're gonna shut down the mine, aren't you?"

"I haven't made a final decision," I said.

I knew Rhys knew I was hedging, but he would give me the grace to do so. Telling him might put him in a tight spot if his grandfather demanded answers from him. It was best for all of us if he could honestly say he didn't know.

"I'll be at your wedding," he commented, shifting topics.

"You will?" I was surprised at that.

"Come on, Archer, don't sound so surprised. If I have a best friend, it's you," he said. "I think of you more like my brother than my cousin."

"Same." My throat felt thick with emotion, and I took a breath. "It'll be good to see you. Are you bringing anyone?"

"Fuck, no."

I could practically imagine his shudder. Rhys dated, and that was it. He didn't even want to get married, or so he claimed. He was scrupulous about not giving anyone the wrong impression.

"If I were to try to bring someone with me, Lord knows what kind of ideas they'd get about that."

I chuckled. "Understood."

"Are you planning to stay in Willow Brook?"

"I might. I'm not sure. It depends on what Phoebe wants. I'll definitely spend a good portion of every year here. It's home to me because I grew up here."

"I know. Your parents wanted you to grow up there because they didn't want you to think the company was everything. They were a hell of a lot smarter than my parents," he said dryly.

"Dude, I'm just as much of a workaholic as you for our family business," I said bluntly.

A laugh rustled in his throat. "True. All right. Give my love to Phoebe and tell her I'll see her at the wedding."

"You got it."

Chapter Seventeen

ARCHER

We were only four days away from the wedding. I was bracing myself for Clint to step up his attacks with the wedding right in front of us. At the same time, I kept shoving those worries to the side.

One morning, I met the interior designer at the house. Amelia and Lucy had moved faster than I'd hoped and finished the updates on the main bedroom and bath, along with the kitchen. They promised they'd work on the rest as well. I'd hired a cleaning crew with the decorating team to follow. They'd polished the floors, cleaned the place thoroughly, and already repainted most of the rooms in neutral colors.

The entire space had a fresh, clean feel. "What do you think, Mr. Cannon?" Vana, the interior decorator, asked.

"I love it," I said, looking around. "And please, just call me Archer."

She nodded. "Of course, Archer. This is really exciting for you."

Glancing her way, I arched a brow. "Falling in love with your childhood best friend, moving back to

Alaska, and getting married. There were some online stories about it. I mean, you are part of Fireweed Industries. Your family is well-known in Alaska and elsewhere," she added.

I bit back a sigh. "Thanks for reminding me. I need to give Phoebe a heads-up."

Vana smiled, her eyes understanding. "Although you two are obviously comfortable with each other, how does she feel about the attention?"

I liked Vana. I didn't sense she had an underlying agenda. She reminded me of many things I liked about Alaska. She was down to earth and took people for who they were as people, not for the labels the world pinned on them.

The typical class lines in Alaska were blurred. Living here meant being self-reliant and also willing to rely on your neighbors. For the most part, people were decent to each other here.

"I don't know how she feels." I shrugged. "She obviously knows my parents were in the family business. But when you're young, you don't think about it much. I'm pretty down to earth, and so is Phoebe. I don't think she'll love the media attention, though."

Vana nodded. "I'm sure she can handle it."

"Thank you for making this happen so fast."

"We wanted you to be able to move in by the wedding. I think you could move in tonight if you'd like. The kitchen crew will be here this afternoon to organize the kitchen. We've made sure there are plenty of linens and towels. If you'd like some assistance with moving, I have a crew that can do it," she offered.

"I don't have much to move. Just my suitcase. I'll have to ask Phoebe if she'd like some help with her apartment."

Vana's phone rang, and she glanced my way, a question in her eyes. "Go ahead and take that," I encouraged.

"If you don't mind, I will."

I gestured toward the doorway, and she slid the phone out of her pocket, walking briskly down the stairs, her voice echoing behind her as she answered.

I slipped my hands into my pockets as I looked around the bedroom. I could imagine living here. The space felt familiar because it was the home I'd grown up in, but the changes created a new feel to it, like it could be mine and Phoebe's. It no longer held the stamp of my parents. I crossed over and sat on the new king-sized bed, bouncing slightly and smiling. The lightweight down quilt was soft gray and paired with plum-colored sheets. The color scheme throughout the room was shades of gray and cream with splashes of color.

I smoothed a palm over the quilt, and my mind flashed to the feel of Phoebe clenching around my fingers and my name on her lips as she came. Lust jolted me. This bed would be ours. I only hoped I could convince her it didn't have to be temporary. Standing, I fished my phone out of my pocket and tapped out a quick text.

Me: *The house is ready. Vana wants to know if you need help with moving your stuff. They have a team. Just say yes. XO*

I smiled as I lowered my hand and walked back out of the bedroom and down the stairs to the living room. Vana was saying goodbye and cast a smile in my direction as she tapped to end her call.

"Do you need me for anything else today?"

"I think I'm all set. Can I text you if Phoebe would like help with moving?"

"Absolutely. Just tell me where and when, and we will make it happen."

"In one day?" I asked lightly.

Vana shrugged. "We have a crew, and we'll bring in extras if needed. You let me know, in the meantime best wishes with your marriage. I hope the wedding goes beautifully."

I thanked her, and she left. My heart had kicked into a rolling drumbeat in my chest. This felt right, but the implications were racing at me. A fist tightened around my heart. I took a breath and let it out. It was supposed to be kind of a joke. We'd get married, and maybe it would be okay, maybe not. I'd hoped the mere presence of Phoebe and the touchstone of our friendship would ease the stress I'd been under lately.

Yet I hadn't expected to fall in love and lust simultaneously.

I walked into the kitchen to glance around. Although the cabinets were empty, I knew they'd be filled within a few hours. Phoebe had been excited about that because she liked to cook. Although she told me she'd be bringing her poached egg pan.

"It might not look as good as the new stuff," she'd offered with a roll of her eyes, "but it's perfect, and that's not something you mess with."

"That'll be our something old," I'd commented.

Her eyes had widened. "What's our something borrowed?"

"Perhaps the marriage itself," I had said, striving to keep my tone casual.

I'd dipped my head and kissed her. "Your eyes are the blue, and we are the new," I'd teased. She'd laughed at the rhyme.

Just then, my phone vibrated in my pocket,

nudging me out of my wandering thoughts. I slipped it out to see her text.

Phoebe: *I hate moving. I'm all about the team handling that. Who do I need to call?*

Me: *I just need to send Vana a text. I'll give them your address. Tell me what time they can meet you there. I'll give her your number so she can call if she needs to follow up on anything.*

I walked out to my SUV to bring in my things. On the upstairs landing, windows ran the length of the wall. They'd furnished it with a lovely desk, some shelving, and a few comfortable chairs. This would be my office, and I settled in to do some work. When my phone rang. I eyed the screen and saw Clint's name flashing. I stared at it, contemplating whether I wanted to answer it or let it go to voicemail.

Avoiding him was usually a wasted effort on my part. If I could've fully cut him out of my life, that would've been different. When I tried to put off dealing with him, dread rose like bile inside.

Standing from my desk, I dragged my thumb across the screen and tapped the speaker button. "Archer here." I began to pace immediately.

"Okay. Listen, you fuck, apparently, my stupid grandson is going to your wedding. I am going to dispute this."

I took a breath, ignoring the tightness building in my chest and the constriction in my throat. "Go ahead. Not much you can do about it. The will is pretty ironclad. I've already talked to the attorney."

"That alone shows you're trying to fake it. Why would you talk to the attorney?" he spit out.

"Because I was prepared to deal with your bullshit," I retorted.

"You're such a little shit. I remember you when

you were a kid. Stupid, always being nice. Wait until I tell her what happened."

"She already knows what happened. I told her. I've known Phoebe for years, and she's my friend."

My pulse was starting to race, and my breath was getting short. Dots formed along the edges of my vision as everything narrowed around me. "I'm not going to talk to you about this," I managed to choke out before I lost my breath completely.

I almost dropped the phone, but I hit the button just in time. I kept my tunnel vision pinned to the phone, confirming that the call had ended. My throat felt too narrow, and I gasped for air, clinging to the edge of my desk as my knees buckled.

The wood surface was cool. I could feel the pounding of my pulse in my palm against it as I clung to my sanity, willing the sense of panic that my great-uncle's voice could evoke to fade. As was always the case when these attacks hit me, I didn't know how long it took. All I knew was that I thought I was going to die until the feeling dissipated.

The tightness in my throat would ease, leaving behind a lingering ache. My lungs would hurt when I gulped in air. When I could finally take a full breath, it would feel as if I was taking in almost too much air because I was so desperate for it. I sank my hips to the floor, sliding my hand over the new carpet and absorbing the feel of it. I leaned my head back, thumping it against the wall.

Fuck. I hated these panic attacks. Back when Clint had more contact with me when I was younger, these didn't happen. The therapist I'd seen for a few months after my doctor referred me said that was a protective mechanism. My hypervigilance was needed to keep me from falling apart. But now, I was safe. Except my nervous system sometimes wasn't sure I was. That was what would trigger the panic, according to my therapist.

Clint was such an asshole. It wouldn't surprise me if he tried to come to the wedding. Once I had enough composure to think, I reached above my head and found my phone on the desk. I pulled up Rhys's number.

Me: *For God's sake, make sure your granddad doesn't dare come to my wedding.*

Rhys: *He's fired up, thinking you're bullshitting. He can't do anything about it.*

Me: *If you find out he might try to come to the wedding, please tell me ASAP.*

Rhys: *I will. The man doesn't even know how to make his own plane reservation. His assistant will fill me in on anything. I'll make sure to check with him. Dude, it's not a secret you guys hate each other.*

My breathing was slowing, and my heart no longer felt as if it was about to break through my ribs. The dots faded from my vision. I stayed on the floor, trying to figure out what the fuck to do.

I needed to get these panic attacks under control. Phoebe was going to be here. My great-uncle's voice was the trigger, but every so often, something else would set me off. That friendly therapist had told me trauma could be a tricky devil. Sometimes it was like grief, where the aftereffects seemed to come out of nowhere. She'd told me to note any events, and I might find a pattern. So far, I'd resisted doing that because I thought I could talk myself out of these panic attacks. Clearly, that wasn't happening.

Chapter Eighteen

PHOEBE

"That looks like it, ma'am," the friendly moving guy said.

The moving crew, all six of them muscley and kind of cute, had moved at warp speed. This one seemed to be the boss.

"Thanks, Dave," I replied. "If you love coffee, the best is right next door at Firehouse Café."

He grinned. "Well, we could use some coffee, but we're also starving."

"Okay, Alpenglow Pizza."

"Where's that?"

"Keep driving down Main Street, and you'll see it on the left."

He dipped his chin in acknowledgment. "You sure you don't need us to get that bag?" His eyes flicked to the backpack sitting by my feet on the floor.

"I can handle my own backpack." I grinned.

"You're a badass, Phoebe," he teased.

"I try to be."

He waited until I stepped out before closing the door behind us. "Vana said to tell you she's sending a cleaning crew over tomorrow, so this will be broom swept for the next tenant."

"Okay, great," I said, my voice coming out kind of squeaky.

I watched as Dave disappeared down the hallway. I stood there alone for a moment before I spun in a small circle. I'd been living here since I moved back to town. I could have stayed with my parents, but that hadn't been my first choice. I loved my parents, but I'd wanted my own space, so this little apartment was perfect for me.

I walked back into the apartment once more, the heels of my cowboy boots echoing on the hardwood floors as I looked around. The moving guys had taken every bit of me out of here. All that was left were the furnishings that came with the apartment. My heart flew into my throat, and butterflies tickled my belly. Moving out of here meant moving in with Archer.

I was conflicted about that. I wanted it almost too much. Our pending marriage was starting to feel *way* too real, and it was stressing me right the hell out.

Every time I thought of the other night with him, I got hot all over. Every cell in my body spun like a fiery pinwheel. I gave my head a shake and left. My phone vibrated as I walked out. I slipped it out of my pocket.

Archer: *Your stuff is here, but you're not. I'd prefer you. I got us some pizza for dinner. I hope you don't mind.*

I smiled down at my phone, tapping out my reply.

Me: *See you in a few. Driving over now.*

I felt almost giddy and then repeatedly chastised myself for that. *Don't get too excited about this. You can't fall for him. Not like this. Sure, he says he wants you, but it's just a little lust between friends.*

Gah! I needed to get a grip, like yesterday.

My hands were sweaty when I came to a stop in the driveway at Archer's house. Considering that snow blanketed the ground, that was ridiculous. Walking into the house felt strange. Memories raced at me as if I was walking through time and seeing my childhood friendship with Archer in photos flashing by.

I sort of calmed down while we ate. Archer took me on a tour, and it was really weird to see all my stuff in the house. Even though I knew the home's layout, it felt different with the new paint and the furnishings. That was a relief. It was confusing enough to be in lust with my childhood best friend.

A glass of wine took the edge off my nerves, and we moved to the living room after dinner. Archer sat at an angle across from me on the sectional. I sensed he was trying to give me a little physical distance so I didn't panic. Annoyance flared inside because I didn't want him to worry. I wasn't the kind of girl who needed to be handled like fine china. I was a hotshot firefighter, for fuck's sake. I could deal with some stress and pressure. That said, jumping from a plane into the wilderness to fight a fire seemed *way* less stressful than the muddied emotional waters I was now navigating with Archer.

"So, everything went okay with the move?" he asked.

"Dude, it was the best move ever. I didn't do anything. Dave—"

"Dave?" Archer prompted, raising one of his brows.

"One of the moving guys," I explained. "He even offered to carry my backpack. Vana is sending a cleaning crew to the apartment tomorrow. I need to call Janet and find out what to do about my lease."

"I've already covered it."

"What?!"

He shrugged as if it was totally no big deal that he'd just paid my rent without asking me. "I didn't want you to worry about it or to leave her in the lurch."

"Archer!" I protested.

"Phoebe," he countered, his tone dry.

"Don't do this. I can't have you taking over like that."

"It's not a big deal."

"But it is for me."

"I know. This is more for Janet than you."

"You're just saying that because you hope I'll accept it then."

"So, what if I am? If it was just some random stranger, I wouldn't care."

I glared at him, forcing myself to take a slow breath while trying to ignore my rising blood pressure.

"Janet said she already had options to rent it next month, and she's considering doing winter vacation rentals to make extra money."

"Yeah, that's a thing here now. That's why it's practically impossible to find rentals around here," I grumbled.

Archer chuckled as he spun his almost empty beer bottle between his fingers. He was leaning forward with his elbows resting on his knees. He was wearing jeans, and his feet were bare. I must've seen his bare feet hundreds of times when I was a kid, but I'd never paid attention. Now, they were man feet, just like his hands. His hands were lean but looked strong. Same thing for his feet, if that could be a thing. Oh, my god. I was seriously considering the sexiness of Archer's feet. I had officially lost my mind.

"So," I began, my voice kind of bright. That was as

far as I got because I had no idea what I meant to say next.

"Soooo?" Archer prompted slowly.

I set my wine glass on the coffee table, making sure to put it on the coaster. This beautiful wooden coffee table was simple with clean lines, and I didn't want to mar the surface. I leaned back into the couch cushions with a sigh, catching the edge of my blouse and sliding it through my fingers.

"I'm nervous," I blurted out. When I didn't know what to do with Archer, I fell back on brutal honesty. "Are you going to tell me I shouldn't be nervous?" I prompted when he didn't say anything else.

His lips twitched with a smile, and his eyes were warm as he shook his head. "No, I find it pointless to tell someone to calm down or that there's no need to be nervous. If I'm nervous when someone tells me I shouldn't be, then I feel kind of ridiculous and get more anxious."

"Yes!"

His smile stretched from one corner of his mouth to the other. My belly tingled, and my pulse shot off as if in a race. "It's just weird, you know. I didn't expect"—I waved my hand vaguely in the air—"any of this. When you texted me, I wanted to see you because even though we hadn't talked very much over the years, you're *that* friend to me. Then you..." I paused, trying to think of the right word.

"Proposed?" Archer offered helpfully.

A nervous laugh slipped out. "Yes, proposed. At first, I was pretty upset with Tasha, and hey, I'm all about saving the environment. It seemed like a good idea, but then you got here, and I didn't expect..." Ugh. I couldn't get a complete sentence out.

He waved his hand in the air between us. "This."

My cheeks heated when I nodded. I bit my bottom lip and closed my eyes, letting out a huff of a laugh when I opened them again. His smoky gaze was waiting for me, watching intently. It felt as if a fuse lit between us, racing from him to me and setting my body alight.

"What is *this* to you?" I asked, ignoring my anxiety.

He looked at me quietly. The heat in his gaze didn't fade, but something else shimmered to life between us. His expression turned serious and intense. I straightened as I tucked my feet under my hips, rubbing the silky edge of my blouse between my fingers. I'd showered earlier and changed into something not completely tomboy—a fitted pair of jeans with flats and a silky blue blouse that Madison insisted made my eyes pop.

I wanted to be more than Archer's old childhood friend. I wanted to be something else other than the tomboyish woman who was a hotshot firefighter.

"*This*, to me, is wanting someone more than I've ever wanted someone before. Needing someone when I never wanted to need anyone before." I swallowed as emotion rushed through me at his words. "And frankly, I want you in my bed. I want to fuck you until you forget everything but me."

My brain cells went up in smoke as tingles radiated throughout my entire body. I could hear every resounding beat of my heart and the rush of blood through my ears as I stared at him. He saved me from having to speak. Considering I was shocked into silence, that was a small win.

"*This*, to me, is wondering just how much this could be because we don't have to do all the hard stuff. When we were growing up, you were my best friend, and coming back has been so easy. I don't trust many people in this world, but you've always been on that very short list. This started for different reasons, but it means a lot more to me now."

I sat in stunned silence while the fierceness of yearning I felt tightened inside.

"Oh." My word was found insubstantial between us, a raspy whisper.

"Was that too much?" Archer asked. "Too honest?"

Wordlessly, I shook my head. It felt as if Archer had come back into my life and walked into my heart, opening all the windows and doors and letting the sunshine flood in. I took a shaky breath.

"What is this to you?" he asked.

Of course, he had every right to ask that. But the question was terrifying because everything felt so big inside. Just having him back in my world felt like more than I ever could have imagined.

"I didn't expect to want you like this. I didn't expect an edge like this, and now, it doesn't feel like a joke. Except maybe on me." I shrugged.

Archer moved swiftly. In a second, he was sitting beside me, his hand sliding over my knee. "None of this is a joke on you, Phoebe," he whispered gruffly.

His mouth descended to mine, and our kiss started slow and searching—a brush of lips, a kiss dropped on one corner of my mouth, and then the other, his hands sliding into my hair, and finally his mouth landing more fully on mine.

I opened for him instantly. Letting Archer into my heart and into my world almost felt impossible to guard against. It felt as if he was learning me. Our kiss was probing—an exploration of tongues tangling, teeth nipping, hot, open, drawing away, words murmured, breaths shared, one liquid moment of need rolling into the next.

The rush of blood pounding in my ears was all I could hear. Archer drew away, his silver-smoke eyes searching mine before skating over my face and dipping down. My nipples tightened at the feel of his gaze. I felt drawn tight, a jumble of sensation and emotion jostling against each other. As much as I wanted Archer—and oh, how I wanted him with a fierceness I couldn't hold back—the wanting was such a force it was as if a dam had cracked. What began as water seeping through slowly had turned into a roar. The gates of the dam long ago lost amidst the froth of the water. I felt raw and exposed because Archer knew me in a way few did. The comfort and familiarity had returned the moment we reconnected. Yet there was now this newness, all of these new emotions, and this depth of need and desire was unfamiliar and over-whelming. I'd never wanted anyone this much. A part of me felt as if I bordered on hysteria because I didn't know what to make of any of this.

Archer's eyes lifted again, his thick lashes sweeping upward. His gaze bored into mine, taking my already tattered breath away.

"What?" I heard myself whisper breathlessly.

He shook his head, just barely. "Nothing."

Somehow, I gathered a sense of composure amidst the tumult of passion and emotion. "I know you, just as you know me. That look wasn't nothing."

His gaze dipped down, and he bit the corner of his lip as a dry laugh rustled in his throat. Once again, I was held in the beam of his gaze. "So true. I suppose I didn't expect this."

I managed to roll my eyes. "Same."

As we stared at each other, that hysteria bubbled over, and I giggled. He laughed with me. In a matter of seconds, I was wiping tears from my eyes. The laughter was a profound relief. The desire hadn't abated, not in the least, but I'd somehow uncapped the lid on my emotions, and that pressure wasn't so intense anymore.

Without thinking, I reached over and languidly trailed my fingertips along his forearm. Sweet Jesus, even his forearms were sexy. The corded muscles were tight under my light touch. I heard the hitch of his breath as I stroked my finger more purposely into the dip of his elbow and over the inside of his bicep.

I managed to take a deep breath, almost as if I were bracing myself. Then I felt the hot shock of his mouth on mine again, and we tumbled into another deep, probing kiss. Layer upon layer of sensation built inside. His hand cupped my nape, and I savored the press of his fingertips before they eased and caressed my skin. Goose bumps rose in the wake of his touch. His fingers were swift and sure as he unbuttoned my blouse.

Cool air struck my skin, and my eyes flew wide open when I let out a gasp. The heat in his eyes nearly undid me. He trailed his knuckles down my breast-bone before unfurling his hand and cupping a breast. His thumb dragged over the taut, achy peak of my nipple. I arched reflexively into his touch, practically purring like a cat. I barely felt like myself. I was driven by fierce, elemental need.

"Archer," I whispered raggedly. "Please."

I didn't even know what I was begging for, but he answered with a nimble flick of his thumb between my breasts. My bra fell open. The sensation of cool air hitting my skin was followed almost instantly by his mouth closing, hot and wet, over a nipple. I speared my fingers in his hair when I cried out again, my hips rocking against his knee, which had somehow found its way between my thighs.

He sucked lightly. I could feel the pull, like an electric sensation, straight from my nipple to my very core. Clenching tightly, I was wet. I shifted my thighs, anxious to do anything to relieve the achy need building there. When he drew away from my nipple, I felt the loss acutely and murmured something in protest.

His low chuckle caused the rush of his breath against my skin just before he turned his attention to my other nipple. Another hot, wet shock, a deep pull, and the sharp graze of his teeth had me crying out. He lifted his head this time.

My greedy side asserted itself. "Shirt off," I ordered.

His smile was quick. Just as I reached for the hem of his shirt, he hooked his hand on the collar behind his head and yanked it off in one swoop.

I swallowed. Oh. My.

Archer's chest was a sight to behold. He was chiseled and cut with a smattering of hair that thinned before it arrowed down behind the waistband of his jeans. I instantly wanted those off. My hands were ahead of my brain as I leaned forward and tugged at the buttons of his fly.

He distracted me temporarily by sliding his palm, his touch warm, over the curve of my belly. Ignoring him, I had his fly unbuttoned in no time and slipped a hand over the hard ridge of his arousal. The heat of it felt like a brand. I was gratified at the sound of his breath hissing through his teeth when he drew in a sharp breath.

I didn't wait before I slid my palm boldly over his length. I was almost startled at how confident I felt. I didn't care for once. My mind wasn't half distracted and dealing with a constant running ticker of what I needed to do.

"Phoebe," he bit out just as I shoved his jeans down far enough to tug his boxers out of the way.

His cock sprang free, and I curled my palm around it. The skin was velvety soft and silky hot. When a bead of cum rolled out the tip, I couldn't resist leaning forward and swiping it up with my tongue.

Archer let out something between a growl and a sound of annoyance. I finally felt like I had the upper hand, even if I knew the feeling was fleeting. I smiled up at him. "Give me a minute," I murmured before I leaned closer and swirled my tongue around the tip.

I sucked him in deep, and his fingers laced roughly in my hair. I savored the subtle sting on my scalp when he choked out my name. I actually giggled—*giggled!*—around the thick length of his cock. A sense of power rolled through me when he murmured, "Phoebe." His tone was laced with warning.

I loved that I could make him feel this way. Drawing back slightly, I teased my tongue along the underside of his cock, dallying just below the thick crown. The length of him pulsed, and I tasted a spurt, the salty tang of his cum dancing over my tongue. His fingers tightened in my hair again when I drew back and sucked him in deeply once more.

I had a hand curled just over the edge of his hip, and I felt his body shift into a shivering tightness before he let out another growl, my name following in a gruff shout as the salty heat of his release filled my mouth.

I waited before slowly drawing away, biting my lip as I looked up at him. His eyes locked with mine. I watched as his breath came in heaves. It felt as if I were watching him pull himself back together. When his eyes darkened, I knew I was in for it.

With one hand, he yanked his jeans back up. He didn't bother to button them, though. In another moment, I found myself spread across the couch as he deftly tugged my jeans down around my hips, dropping hot kisses over my belly. He murmured teasing, commanding words, and I shivered all over.

"You're mine now. Just you wait."

His hand curled over the edge of my panties, dragging them down while I kicked my jeans free. I cried out when I felt his fingers parting my folds and sliding inside me knuckle deep. My cry was a ragged whimper.

Chapter Nineteen

ARCHER

I looked down at Phoebe, her honey-gold locks in a tousle on the couch cushions. Her nipples were pink and damp. Her belly trembled as she breathed raggedly.

My breath bellowed, and my heart kicked like an echoing drum with every cell in my body reverberating to the rush of it. Her pussy clenched around my fingers. She was wet, so silky and soft. Leaning over, I gave in to the temptation to tease one of her nipples, my lips closing around it. I gave it a sharp suck, and her body bowed toward me.

She murmured my name, the sound of it pleading. To be fair, I turned my attention to her other nipple. I wouldn't want it to feel left out. I smiled against her skin when she protested, "Archer."

Her tone was demanding and breathy. I loved that I could bring tough firefighter Phoebe to the point of pleading with me. I teased my fingers through her slippery folds, exploring, letting my thumb just glance over her clit. I mapped her belly with my lips—a kiss, a nip, lingering over the trembling surface. She was fit

—strong and sturdy. Yet somehow, she was so feminine and soft. She couldn't hide the lush give of her hips and the soft curves of her breasts.

Her skin was flushed pink with a dewy sheen. Despite the fact she'd just brought me to a searing release, I was enthralled by her, twisted tightly with need.

Yet I'd made a promise to myself. Maybe what we were doing was crazy. Maybe I was risking one of the best friendships I'd ever had in my life. But I was going to save one thing for our wedding night.

I sank my fingers deep inside her, stretching and testing. Finally, *finally*, I let myself taste her. I already knew the tease of it after cleaning her arousal off my fingers the last time. I hooked one of her knees under my hand as I lifted it, baring her to me. She was pink and quivering. I blew lightly on her sex, a sizzle of satisfaction jolting me when she trembled and her fingers clenched into the couch cushion beneath her.

I licked into the very core of her. Her hips bucked roughly under my touch, so I gripped her hip to hold her steady. Fuck, she tasted good—salty and tangy. I dallied, letting my tongue draw a lazy circle around the swollen bud of her clit. I loved every sound she made —these little whimpers and ragged cries interspersed with my name and then, oh my god, please.

I could only draw it out for so long because Phoebe was magnificent like this, the way her body flexed under my touch, the way she trembled and shivered. I fucked her with my fingers, lifting my eyes to watch as she got closer and closer to the edge, and then demanded, "Archer. Now!"

Once again, I dipped my head and sucked lightly on her clit when I buried my fingers inside her. She drew tight and then shuddered roughly, my name following her keening cry. I stayed with her until she relaxed underneath me.

When I lifted my head, my heart kicked up its speed again, and my breath caught in my throat. Phoebe bare before me, flushed and strong, replete in her passion, was a sight to behold. I slowly drew my fingers out of her and shifted upward. I slid between her and the back of the couch, and she curled against me, soft and warm.

My heart was still pounding in a restless beat. Thundering emotions rushed through me like a storm. I smoothed her hair away from her face, forcing myself to look at her even though I was almost afraid. I feared what she might see in my eyes. Her gold-tipped lashes lifted, and she rolled her head to the side. We stared at each other quietly.

"Well," she whispered.

"Well," I repeated, curling my lips into a smile.

She returned my smile, but after a moment, her gaze sobered. She lifted a hand, tracing her fingers lightly along my collarbone before rocking her hips slightly against me. She opened her mouth, starting with, "We should go to the bedroom."

"We can, but we're sleeping," I said, my words coming out firm.

She blinked. "Why?"

"I told you. I want to save one thing for our wedding night."

My stomach tightened up at being honest, but I'd already been honest, so I might as well stay with it.

"It's silly," she said, her mouth twisting a little.

"Maybe, but it's one thing to save just for us."

"Should I remind you this all started as a marriage of convenience? Some people might even say it's fake," she pointed out.

"Maybe that's why it started, but the way I feel isn't fake at all. Tell me the way you feel is," I said bluntly, holding her gaze.

Pink crested high on her cheeks, and she shook her head. "I'm not going to lie."

"I'm not sleeping alone. By the time the wedding rolls around, we won't be able to wait, and it'll be a miracle if we make it through more than a few minutes of the reception."

Phoebe giggled, and the sound spun around my heart.

"Nothing else is off-limits, just sex?" she clarified.

"Just the full act. That's all."

When I slid my hand over her belly, I realized she had goosebumps. "You're cold."

"I'm half-naked," she pointed out.

I rolled to a sitting position as she straightened. I wanted to bundle her into my arms, take her to bed, and forget my ridiculous idea about saving sex for our wedding night.

"They've already unpacked your clothes," I commented.

"They did?" She looked surprised.

At my nod, she leaped up and hurried across the living room.

Damn. The sight of her lush bottom bouncing as she strode quickly away from me sent a jolt of blood straight to my cock. This was going to be an interesting four days.

Chapter Twenty

PHOEBE

I was warm—so, *so* warm—and I burrowed closer into the source of the heat. The sound of my own sleepy, happy sigh woke me. My awareness came in fragments. It was dark when my eyes blinked open. My palm was resting on someone's chest. The haze of sleep faded, and awareness clicked into place.

That warm, hard chest belonged to Archer. The events of the night before came rushing back. My skin prickled, and my body crackled with awareness and recognition. The memories were grounded in sensation—all of it good and all of it unsettling.

I was curled up, practically latched on to Archer like a barnacle. My knee was thrown over his thigh, my breasts were mushed against the side of his chest, and my head was tucked into the curve of his shoulder. As much as I didn't want to admit it or really even contemplate it, it felt so good. I was so often cold when I slept that I had resigned myself to that reality.

I loved my home state of Alaska, but it meant cold winters, and February was the coldest time of the year. We were deep into winter with everything holding tight to stay warm enough to survive. Although humans had heat and housing, I still believed our primal instincts kicked in. My body knew winter was cold, no matter how many blankets I had.

Archer was the best source of heat *ever*. We weren't completely naked. He was wearing a pair of boxers, and I wore a tank top and a soft pair of leggings, which Archer teased me about sleeping in until I told him I always got cold. His lips had kicked up at one corner in a lazy smile when he replied, "I don't think you'll be cold. I'm always hot."

I smiled to myself in the darkness. He was generous with his warmth, and it was free. It wasn't like turning up the heat and dealing with a high bill. Of course, there were potential consequences to my sanity, our friendship, and my heart. That price might be more than I could ever pay. I mentally scurried away from that train of thought.

I almost jumped when I heard Archer's voice. "You okay?"

His voice was rumbly and soft, the mere sound of it ruffling my nerves a little. I was trying to get used to his effect on me, but it was strange. I kept thinking I'd somehow lapse back into not thinking Archer was the hottest man ever known to the universe. No such luck yet.

"Phoebe?" he prompted, his voice a little clearer this time.

"I'm fine," I replied.

I lifted my head reluctantly from the warm curve of his shoulder to eye the clock on the nightstand beside the bed. The digital numbers blinked in a silver glow at me.

"It's four thirty, isn't it?" he asked.

"How did you know?"

The rustle of his laughter in the darkness sent heat prickling over my skin. "I always wake up at four thirty. I thought I might break myself of the habit being back here in Alaska, but it's not happening."

I smiled at him as I curled my palm into a fist and rested my chin on top of it on his chest. "I tend to get up at five, a whole half hour later."

"I don't know, Phoebe, that doesn't seem early enough to me," he teased.

I nudged my elbow lightly into his chest. "Five *is* early. Don't even argue with me about this."

His palm slid up my back from where it had been resting just above the curve of my bottom, and he began to slide his fingers through my hair. I felt like a cat about to purr at his casual, easy touch. "Okay, I won't argue with you," he replied.

"Have we ever argued?" I asked, honestly wondering.

"I don't think so."

My eyes had adjusted, and I could see his face in the darkness from the pearly light cast from the night-light at the foot of the bed.

"I can't remember a single argument, not even about dumb stuff," I said.

His smile was like a little gift I wanted to snatch and hold close to my heart. "I can't think of any fights we had. If we're getting married, maybe we should practice."

"Practice fighting?"

"Yeah," he replied.

"Why? What would we have to fight about? That's one of the reasons I think we're such good friends. We just get along. You're not really an argumentative person."

"Well, neither are you, but I think most couples fight about something."

"Perhaps." I rolled my eyes.

"Don't roll your eyes," he returned, his chest rumbling with a barely-there laugh.

"There. That was a fight," I teased.

When I shifted, my knee brushed against his arousal. That subtle touch sent a zing of electricity through me, radiating outward from my knee.

"Ignore it," Archer ordered.

Flustered, I shifted my leg again even though I had already snatched it back. "Okay, I'll try." I felt my cheeks heat at how raspy and squeaky my voice sounded.

"It's morning wood," he offered matter-of-factly.

"Is that really a thing?"

His eyes met mine in the almost darkness, and I felt his shoulders shift in a shrug under me. "Yes and no. Sometimes, guys just wake up like that. I don't really need to do anything about it. It goes away. And then sometimes, I wake up and need to do something about it."

My question slipped out before I could think better of it. "Which one is this?"

He chuckled as his fingers slid up to tease along the downy skin at the back of my neck. I was awash in goose bumps, and my belly felt light and tingly.

"This is one I'd like to do something about, but we're not doing anything about it," he said firmly.

"We're not?" I was incredulous and unbelievably aroused. I could feel the slick heat between my thighs and had to shift my legs slightly to relieve the restless, needy ache.

"Because I won't make it to the wedding if we're making out all the time."

I pressed my lips together, glaring at him. "I think this is kind of ridiculous."

"I don't."

"Isn't it going to be worse if we don't do anything?"

"We've got three more nights to get through. We can't be at it all the time."

"I think it's ridiculous," I repeated.

"Why?" His question came out raspy and somber.

I suddenly felt uncertain and uncomfortable. "I don't know."

"Maybe this whole idea was convenience at the beginning, but it's not anymore."

"Maybe," I hedged.

"Are you going to start pretending now?" he asked bluntly.

My heart fluttered, and a sense of tingling lightness stole through me. I took a quick breath of air, needing the oxygen to steady me. "No," I whispered.

Just when I thought I couldn't take it anymore, his fingers slipped into my hair. He drew me closer, bringing his mouth to mine in a kiss almost lazy and so sensual I melted against him. By the time we broke apart, my entire body was pulsing with need and pounding a hard fist against the door of my willpower.

"Archer, that's not fair," I gasped.

"To you or me?" he asked dryly.

He sounded composed, but I could feel the rapid beat of his heart under my palm where it was splayed against his chest.

"Tell me everything I missed," he prompted.

"What do you mean?"

"Let's see, we were best friends all the way until I moved away. I sent you a few letters, and you sent me a few. I know that you played basketball."

I smiled, my forehead falling to his chest as I

shook with laughter. Lifting my head, I took a breath. "I did. I was pretty good. Not good enough for college, though."

"That's what I mean. I missed a lot."

I found myself filling Archer in on my life, and we traded details about each other. Like the little notes we used to send in elementary school, back when everything seemed so much simpler.

We never did fall back asleep. Finally, Archer tugged me out of bed, persuading me to take a shower with him. Apparently, showering with him involved bringing me to an orgasm against the tiled wall and leaving me nearly boneless. Steam rose around me with my palms flat against the tile as I tried to catch my breath while sensations ricocheted through every corner of my body.

"I thought you said we shouldn't do that too much," I managed after I caught my breath.

When I looked at him, he was fully aroused. He shrugged. "I meant me, not you." At that, he turned off the water and stepped out of the shower.

By the time I gathered my composure and enough strength to follow him, he already had on a pair of jeans and was tugging a T-shirt over his delectable chest.

"Do you want to have coffee here, or should we go to Firehouse?" he asked when his head appeared through the neck of his shirt, and he pulled it down over his abs. The fact that shirts hid his abs was a huge disappointment for me, but I'd have to live with it.

"Do we have groceries and things here?" I asked.

"Of course, we do."

I was discovering there were benefits to Archer's wealth. "I had the moving team do a grocery run for us. My assistant sent them a list."

"Assistants handle grocery lists?" I asked, eyeing him skeptically.

"All the time." His lips twitched.

I rolled my eyes. "What do you prefer?"

"I'm fine with either. There could be a benefit to us going to Firehouse. We can mention that we've moved in together, that sort of thing."

My pulse became unsteady, and I took a shaky breath. "Wow. All of... this."

"What's this?" he interjected.

I circled my hand in the air. "I don't know, making sure people know what's going on. It feels more like we're trying to put on a show, and it's fake."

"It's real." His tone was firm and confident.

I still had a towel wrapped around me when Archer crossed over to me. His hands landed on my shoulders, sliding down and coming to rest on my hips. He dipped his head and pressed a quick kiss on my lips. "It can be both because, originally, it was a convenience thing. You're going to save the planet or at least this one river in Alaska. I was going to make your ex and your old friend feel like the assholes they are. Now, I don't think you care so much about your ex and your old friend."

I shook my head. "Not really. I do care about the planet, though. I still care about that."

The sharp bark of his laugh ricocheted in my chest. "Is that funny?"

"Yes and no. Just like fake and real can exist. Of course, you want to save the planet. You're that kind of person. It's just a funny situation," he explained.

"We should go to town," I decided.

"This is real for me, and my family also needs to believe it."

"Do they really care?"

"Most of them don't. My great-uncle does, though. He would love to maintain control of the company." Archer's lips twisted, and something dark flickered in his eyes like the shadows of leaves when the wind blows.

He moved away quickly, turning and grabbing a flannel shirt to shrug into. I got dressed in a pair of jeans with a fitted V-neck shirt. When I turned, he was waiting in the doorway. His eyes skated over me.

"I like that shirt," he commented.

I looked down. "It's just a shirt. There's nothing special about it."

"If it's you, there is. Plus..." He pushed away from the door without a word, crossing to me in three quick strides. "I love this." His knuckles trailed lightly over the exposed skin between my breasts. His touch felt like fire over my skin. The air around us heated instantly.

"Oh," I rasped.

His touch was gone as quickly as it came. My stomach rumbled, and he grinned. "Hungry?"

"Yes, I like breakfast," I said a little defensively.

Chapter Twenty-One

PHOEBE

"How is the house?" Janet asked as soon as we reached the front of the line.

"It's great," I replied. "Money can't buy happiness, but it does make moving easier."

Janet chuckled, and Archer grinned.

"A crew moved all my stuff. I've never had that happen," I added.

"Good. You deserve to be taken care of," Janet said with a firm nod.

That was what it felt like with Archer, that he would take care of everything, including me. I liked feeling independent and not needing anyone. I mentally skittered away from savoring that feeling and focused on Janet. "I didn't even pack anything. They did everything for me. Lord knows what they thought of my underwear."

"You probably wear cotton," Janet offered with a wink.

Heat raced up my cheeks. Archer squeezed my hand because he knew I wore cotton and silk.

"What'll it be?" Janet prompted.

"I want that special you made me the other day," Archer said. "No sugar."

"I hate sugar in my coffee," I interjected. "You know what I prefer, just the house coffee with an extra shot."

"Your girl keeps it simple," Janet offered as she smiled over at Archer and began to prep our coffees.

His smile felt like a ray of sun coming out from behind a cloud, and I felt myself practically beaming at him. Oh. My. God. He'd turned me into a ridiculous crusher.

Just then, I heard someone coming in, and I glanced over to see my ex-friend Tasha. Her face was tight. She stopped in the back of the line, lifting her hand in a small wave. I nodded in return. Archer was saying something to Janet about coffee. She finished ringing us up, and we snagged a table in the corner. I could feel the burn of Tasha's cold gaze on me from across the café.

After a sip of my coffee, I commented, "She hates me, and I'm not even the one who put us in this position."

Archer shrugged. "No, you're not, but that's not how it works."

"What do you mean?"

"People who do shitty things don't usually feel bad about it. Sometimes it's easier to blame it on somebody else."

"Are you a human nature expert?" I teased.

He chuckled. "Definitely not. But I've seen it play out enough in my life. She's headed this way," he warned.

"That's fine," I said as I looked over. "I might as well have a conversation with her." I smiled politely when she stopped beside our table. "Hi, Tasha."

My smile did feel a little tight, but I *really* was okay. The whole thing stung a little, mostly because I'd thought she was the kind of friend who had my back. Instead, she was doing things behind my back.

"You know, if you did this to make me feel like shit, I just want you to know you did," she said.

"What?" I sputtered.

"Aren't you the one who did something?" Archer interjected pointedly.

Tasha's cheeks turned a ruddy shade of pink, her fingers curling tightly around her coffee cup. "I did. I know I screwed up, but practically no one wants to come to my wedding."

"How is that my fault?" I countered.

"Because your wedding is way more exciting. It was on some gossip website."

"We had nothing to do with that." I wasn't going to admit to her Archer's original proposal might've been partially because he knew my pride had taken a few kicks. That wasn't what it was about anymore. "Tasha, I'm not trying to hurt you," I finally said.

"Okay, well, I wasn't trying to hurt you either," she insisted.

"Well, you did. You know it's really not about Dirk. It's about you screwing around with him behind my back and lying to me. That's not what friends do."

She sighed. "I know." She ran her hand over her hair roughly. I knew she was flustered because she had been my friend before. "Look, I fucked up. Okay, I really did." Her throat worked with a swallow. "We're calling off the wedding."

"You are?" This startled me. Tasha was pretty stubborn, and getting married was a big deal for her.

"Here's the shitty thing. You said it when you found out about us. If he cheated before, he'll do it again. I can't get out of my own way even though I'm the one who put myself in this position," she said, her voice sounding choked.

"Tasha, I'm sorry." Pushing my chair back, I stood quickly and pulled her into a hug.

She was stiff, but after a moment, she relaxed, and I could feel her shudder and knew she was trying not to cry. My heart pinched. Stepping back, I squeezed her shoulders before my hands fell away. "I know getting married is a big thing for you, the wedding, the whole deal."

She swallowed again, blinking rapidly. "Yeah, and I kind of can't really feel good about it when I put myself in this position."

The urge to apologize was right there in my throat. I felt myself wanting to tip into it, but this part wasn't my fault. "You're welcome to come to our wedding," I offered.

"I know, but I think that's kind of weird. I haven't been a good friend," she said, finally saying aloud the part that had hurt me so.

"I understand. Are you staying in town?"

Tasha took a quick swallow from her coffee. I felt as if I was watching her batten down her hatches. She straightened her spine and pushed her shoulders back. "I don't think so. I'm going to stay through tomorrow, but I've already booked a flight. If you're ever in Seattle, I'd love to see you."

Tasha turned and looked at Archer. "I wasn't here when you lived here, but I know you're Phoebe's oldest friend. It's really awesome you guys are together."

Archer cocked his head to the side, his eyes assessing before he nodded slowly. "I think you mean that," he said slowly.

"I do. I fucked up. I'm sorry, I really am," she whispered.

She turned to go, but I caught her by the elbow. When she looked back, I offered, "I'm sorry it didn't work out for you."

She sucked in a breath and took another sip of coffee before she nodded. "I appreciate that. I don't expect it to happen overnight and realize we may never get back to the kind of friends we were before, but just let me know if you ever need anything. I can tell you one thing I've learned from this."

"What's that?"

"Your friends are more important than someone else who tempts you to think it's okay to screw them over." She gave me a fierce hug, and I squeezed her back, then watched as she walked out of the café.

I sat down slowly, meeting Archer's eyes. "Well, that sucks that she's not getting married."

"No, but I think it makes sense," he commented.

"I'm just sorry she's hurt."

"You're a really good friend, Phoebe." Archer's gaze was so intent, my heart kicked in response.

"You are too."

He smiled. "You know they say the most important part about marriage is having a solid base. I think we have that."

My lips curled into a smile. "You do?"

"Yes. You're a good friend, and I'm a good friend. I can promise you I wouldn't do anything like what Tasha did."

I sighed. "I don't really know what led her to do it."

"Sex?" he prompted dryly.

"Dirk wasn't even that good in bed." My hand flew to my mouth as I gasped.

Archer waggled his brows. "No?"

"Archer," I warned.

His tongue pushed into the corner of his mouth as he cast me a sideways grin.

I sighed again. "You didn't really need to know that, but no."

"Yeah, but maybe he was for her. Plus, there's always the thrill factor. I wouldn't know anything about it, but we all have a friend who screwed around on somebody. The forbidden has its temptations," he observed.

"I suppose. Well, now it's all about the environment," I added dryly.

He reached for my hand, lifting it and dropping a kiss in the center of my palm. "I think that's worthy, but more than that, you're worthy."

We smiled at each other just as his phone rang where it was sitting on the table. He spun it to look down. Once again, I felt as if I watched shadows pass through his gaze. His expression was careful when he looked up at me, and I knew he didn't want me to wonder what he was thinking. "What is it?"

Chapter Twenty-Two

ARCHER

"I told you he was pissed," Rhys said later that day.

I adjusted one of my earbuds. "Yeah, he sure is."

"He's really pissed Phoebe's your old friend. He actually said that makes it seem real," my cousin added.

"It *is* real," I practically growled.

I would never tell anyone how it started with Phoebe and me because that was beside the point now.

"Please make sure he does not show up at the wedding."

"I will. It's a long flight. I don't think he'd want to go anyway."

"Has he ever been here?" I asked.

"I don't think so. I came to visit a few times when your parents lived there, but he always said it was too far."

"Does he seriously think I'm going to run this branch of the company into the ground? I've already told you my plans."

"I know. You know he's cynical as hell. He can't look at the long run, so he's just digging his heels in."

"Look, Off the Grid, the alternative energy company down in Diamond Creek, is making money hand over fist. They're a leader. I'm going to partner with them, and we're going to reconfigure everything. We don't need to mine. It's unnecessary."

"You'll have to make a serious investment," Rhys warned.

"I know, and we have the money."

"I know."

"So, I'm going to see you this weekend, right?" I asked.

"I wouldn't miss it. If my granddad shows up, I'll kick him out."

After we finished the call a few minutes later, I set my phone on my desk. I looked out over the view. It was so familiar, and I loved it, yet it all felt fresh and new. My emotions felt sharp, the edges of them crisp. The mountains were covered in snow, jagged and bright against the blue sky.

I looked at my phone screen again and opened my voicemail. I'd been putting off listening to my great-uncle's voicemail solely because I hated the sound of his voice. That familiar dread curled in my stomach, but I tapped the message to listen because I refused to avoid him completely.

So, Rhys tells me it's your childhood friend. So romantic. What the fuck? You're nothing but a coward. You know it, and I know it.

The urge to flee rose inside, prickling up my spine. I held the memories at bay, clenching my jaw against the panic that started to swell.

I hope it lasts. It's a good thing your grandmother loves you, just like she loves your parents.

The line went dead. At that sound, I swallowed. It was a solid five minutes before I got the panic under control.

Chapter Twenty-Three

ARCHER

Phoebe stood at the kitchen counter. She was wearing a pair of leggings with these fluffy purple socks and a pink sweater that hung down to her hips. Everything about her was soft, and I wanted to slide my hands under that sweater, over her silky skin, and tease her nipples until they were tight little peaks.

"How do you like them?" she asked.

I was a little slow to reply to her question.

"So?" she prompted.

I masked my lustful reverie by taking a quick swallow of my beer. "How do I like what?"

My fiancée pressed her lips together, her ponytail swinging as she shook her head. "How do you like your eggs? Scrambled, over easy, or poached. We have a really nice poach pan."

"I love poached eggs."

"You do?" Her lips spread into a smile.

It was two nights before our wedding, and I was about to lose my mind. I was regretting my stupid plan to save sex. I mean, really? Did it actually matter? The downside was I was feeling stubborn because we'd made it this far. We only had two more nights.

Phoebe's smile sent my heart into a flip in my chest. I had gone from lusting after her to falling for her so hard and fast I didn't even know how to face it. I kept thinking I could manage it, telling myself it wasn't insane because we'd known each other forever. I didn't remember life without knowing Phoebe. In the years we hadn't been in geographical proximity and had grown apart, her absence had been acute the entire time.

Still oblivious to my train of thought, she said, "Poached eggs, it is."

She spun away and fetched her nice poaching pan that she'd mentioned when she moved in.

"I've never had beer and eggs together," I commented as I stood from where I'd been sitting on the opposite side of the kitchen island.

She opened the refrigerator and fetched a carton of eggs. "Are there rules about that?" she asked.

"I don't think so." I finished my beer and crossed over to rinse the empty bottle in the sink and put it in the recycling bin underneath.

When I turned back, she asked, "How many?"

"Four. Are you going to have any?"

"Yes, I'm the one who wanted eggs," she replied, giving me a skeptical side-eye.

"Are you going to poach yours too?"

She blinked, eyeing the poaching pan, which had six poaching spots. "Yes."

"Do you like poached eggs?" I teased lightly.

Her lips twisted as she shrugged. "You know I do. That's why I have a favorite pan."

I couldn't resist anymore. I walked over, resting my

hands on either side of her on the counter. She blinked up at me before her eyes slid to the egg carton on the counter just beyond where one of my hands was resting.

"I was going to make eggs. I'm cooking."

"Not yet," I murmured.

I dipped my head, nuzzling into the sweet curve of her neck. I heard the subtle sound of her breath hitching, and lust sizzled through me. I tried to grab the reins of my control, but they slipped loose. I needed to taste her. She smelled so sweet.

I pressed hot, open kisses along the side of her neck, savoring when she trembled slightly in my arms and arched into my touch.

"Archer," she said breathlessly.

"Hmm?" I murmured against her skin.

She shivered. "I'm cooking." Her voice came out in a whimper.

I lifted my head. "I can't wait."

I couldn't resist kissing her. One of her hands landed on my chest as the other slid up around my nape and tugged me closer. Her tongue danced out to tease with mine. Within a single second, I was on fire for her, hard and desperate.

I slid my hand under her sweater, gliding over the soft curve of her waist to lightly cup her breast. With just the lightest touch, I traced my thumb over her nipple. She gasped into our kiss before breaking free and taking in sharp pulls of air.

"Two more nights. And we already—" She stopped abruptly to suck in more air.

"We already what?" I prompted.

Her cheeks flushed pink. "Well, I mean, there was this morning in the shower," she murmured.

This morning in the shower was amazing. I'd teased her to a climax with my fingers. And then she'd knelt in front of me and sucked me off. I'd come all over her chest before dragging her to her feet and washing it all off.

"What else?" I prompted again when she didn't elaborate.

Her eyes narrowed as her blush deepened. "You know what I mean."

Phoebe wasn't shy with me, but she was shy talking about it. I loved it. I moved my hand regretfully away from her breast.

"We can make it two nights. Don't you think?" she asked.

I dragged in a breath. "Yes."

"Are we spending tomorrow night together?"

I eyed her. "Yes. Why are you asking?"

She shrugged. "There's that superstition about seeing each other the day of the wedding thing. If we wake up together, then we'll see each other."

"Do you really think that means anything?" I *really* didn't want to spend a night apart from her, even if being with her was a form of torture.

"I don't know."

"Maybe we should." I heard myself saying while my body practically screamed aloud in protest. "Where are you going to stay?"

"I can stay with my parents."

"Or I can stay at a hotel," I offered.

She shimmied out from under one of my arms, shaking her head. "This is your house."

Phoebe went and made us the poached eggs. I woke in the middle of the night hours later. I was curled up behind her, my cock hard and aching, nestled against her lush bottom. Fuck me.

Rolling to the side, I glanced at the clock. It was two in the morning. I told myself I should run away from her and go take a cold shower. But if all I could have at this moment was to be curled up against her, I would take it. I didn't know how, but I managed to fall back asleep.

Chapter Twenty-Four

PHOEBE

"You look beautiful." My mother smoothed her hands over my shoulders as she stood behind me.

I stared at myself in the mirror. I had never been one of those girls who dreamed about my wedding. Oh sure, I'd wanted to find love. But here I was, having a wedding with a photographer and everything.

Archer insisted on it, saying if we didn't do that, then we'd be stuck with bad photos in the media. He told me this way we managed the narrative. Whatever that meant. My belly was all fluttery, and my pulse kept thrumming along at high speed.

Madison had planned an actual wedding for me. She promised me it would be beautiful. She'd even dragged me out dress shopping. I'd gone with whatever she suggested, which turned out to be a cream silk slip. It rested at the tops of my shoulders before dipping into a curve in the front with the top of my back exposed. It was fitted but not too tight.

Madison had done my hair, insisting I had to have someone do it. She was good at many things, I had discovered. She'd pulled it up into an artful twist, somehow pinning it with only a few pins. She'd pulled out some locks to frame my face and insisted on a little hair spray.

"I don't wear hair spray," I'd announced.

"I don't care. You need it. You can't have your hair fall down in the middle of your wedding," she'd countered.

My mother turned me around. "I love this."

"My dress?"

Her lips curled in a warm smile. "Your dress is lovely, but I'm talking about you and Archer. You two were the best of friends before, the kind of friends not everyone gets in life. Now you're getting married, and I see the way he looks at you."

"What do you mean?"

"He loves you, and he really gets you." She squeezed my shoulders before her hands fell away.

My breath was shaky when I drew it in. "Is this crazy? Is it too soon?"

"No, not at all. You've known Archer longer than any friend you've ever had. Maybe you haven't seen each other for a while, but it's not too soon."

"A while is over a decade, Mom."

Her eyes were understanding and way too percep-tive. "Sweetie, it's okay."

"Is it really, though? Am I crazy?" I sort of repeated myself.

"I guess we're all a little crazy when it comes to love, but are you crazy to marry Archer? No. You know him far better than many people know each other when they get married."

"But he's wealthy now."

My mom shrugged. "And his parents were wealthy when he was a little boy. It didn't matter then, and it doesn't matter now. Money doesn't define a person. If it does, then you don't want to marry them."

I took a shaky breath. "And what if...?"

My mother's hands landed on my shoulders again. She squeezed gently before her touch slid down my arms. "What if, what if, what if? There are thousands of what-ifs in any marriage. If you really want to back out, I will support you, but I don't think that's what's happening. I think you're afraid because Archer really means something to you."

My heart felt too big for my chest with emotion swelling into my throat. I nodded without even thinking. My mother knew me well, and she was exactly right.

Her eyes shifted beyond my shoulder. "You have five minutes, and I need to go get seated. Your father is waiting to walk you down the aisle. Shall I walk you out to the entryway?"

I gulped in a breath and nodded. All of my what-ifs and doubts were bouncing against each other, but I didn't want to back out of this. *That* might've been the most terrifying part of all.

Only two months prior, I hadn't been engaged. Now, I was engaged to marry my best friend. I walked out with my mother and watched as she disappeared through the wooden doorway into the front of the church. My father's eyes twinkled as he looked down at me.

"Are you ready, dear?"

"You almost never call me dear," I returned.

"Well, now seems like the time to call you that. I love you, Phoebe," he said solemnly.

"Oh, my god, Dad." Emotion coursed through me, and I sucked in a breath, trying not to cry. "I love you too."

He slipped his arms around my shoulders, squeezing me in a quick hug. "Phoebe, girl, let's do this," he said when he stepped back. "I trust Archer, and I know he'll be good to you. Are you ready?"

My chin was dipping in a nod before I could think. It was as if my body knew the answer even though my mind was confused and my heart was vulnerable.

I never meant to fall in love with Archer. Oh, I had already loved him the way you love an old friend, the kind of friend he'd always been to me. But this?

Willow Brook was crowded with wedding guests and even a news truck from Anchorage. This was madness.

The next half hour passed in a blur. It was almost an out-of-body experience. Except for when we said our vows. Archer had wanted to adjust them.

Among other things, he said, "I will cherish and love you as the best friend you've always been. Now, we take the next step in our lifelong friendship."

The words were so true, and it felt so real. I remembered his eyes, silver smoke, staring at me, and my heart feeling as if the doors had been kicked open. I couldn't hide behind them anymore, not with him.

I remembered his lips meeting mine and the electric shock reverberating through my system when he dipped me into a real kiss. I was breathless by the time we broke apart. Then I was giggling, and it was all okay, and now I was married.

I met a jumble of people from his family, many of whom I'd met before. Sometime later in the reception, his cousin Rhys smiled down at me, so similar to Archer.

"Well, Phoebe, here you are stealing Archer's heart. Although maybe you've always had it," Rhys said.

I managed to smile, offering, "Maybe."

The reception continued, and I carried on in a haze. Madison had succeeded wildly, somehow finding the perfect balance for the wedding I wanted, or rather the wedding I hadn't known I wanted. The reception was catered by Firehouse Café and the new pizza place, and the food was delicious. It had a casual feel with a touch of formal to it. She'd found a local band and deejay, and there was fun and dancing.

The only thing that marred the evening was the unexpected appearance of Archer's great-uncle.

I'd never met the man, unlike some of Archer's other family who had come up to visit when we were kids. The second I heard his voice, my spine stiffened. Archer's hand had been resting on my hip, curled around the edge as he laughed at something.

"Archer," his cousin Rhys said, a hint of warning in his tone.

I felt the press of his fingertips when he tensed at my side. I knew him so well. When I looked up into his eyes, I could've sworn I saw a flash of panic skip through his gaze. His eyes closed for longer than a blink, but just barely. His great-uncle stood across from us.

"I understand congratulations are in order," the man said.

I looked at Archer before my gaze bounced to his cousin. He stood in a slouch, his eyes narrow. "I don't think you were invited to the wedding, Granddad." His tone was light, but it was laced with a sharp edge.

"I wasn't. I'm crashing the reception. After all, Archer will be taking over the entire division I manage. I might as well do a last check-in before he officially takes over," he explained.

No one had introduced him. I just sensed that was who he was.

"What the hell are you doing here?" Archer's grandmother barked. She wheeled over in her wheelchair.

Archer's hand was still on my waist, but his touch had gone stiff. His fingertips were pressing into me hard enough that I was concerned.

When Archer's great-uncle looked toward his grandmother, I glanced up at him, sliding my palm over to lace into his fingers and carefully bring his hand off my hip. "Are you okay?" I whispered, turning to him.

He gave an imperceptible nod. "Fine."

Archer's great-uncle was fully focused on his grandmother. Rhys glanced at us, leaning toward me. "Get Archer out of here," he whispered, low and clear in my ear.

"I need to use the bathroom," I said to Archer. "Walk with me, please."

Archer stared down at me, and I could tell my request had puzzled him, but he went along. I led him through the crowd, his hand stiff and cold in mine. He was quiet and seemed caught in a shuttered space inside his own head. Someone stopped to congratulate us, and it seemed to snap Archer out of whatever was going on in his mind.

It was my friend Jonah, another firefighter. He was a funny guy. He and Archer had hit it off when they bonded over their shared love of the recent influx of breweries in Alaska.

"When are you two gonna disappear? I mean..." Jonah glanced at his watch, waggling his eyebrows as he looked up.

I laughed as Archer flashed a grin, seeming almost back to himself. "Soon, very soon."

Jonah clapped Archer on the shoulder as he continued by, aiming for the cake table in the front. I kept my fingers tightly laced into Archer's as we walked toward the hallway on the far side where the restrooms were.

I was relieved when the door to the hallway swung shut behind us, muting the voices. A server passed by with a tray of champagne, offering congratulations. When I got to the sign that indicated the women's restroom, I still didn't release Archer's hand. I pulled him in with me before closing and bolting the door.

He looked around. "What if someone else needs to come in?"

There were three stalls. "They can wait. I'm the bride, so nobody will mind if we make out in here. Are you okay?" I turned to face him, reaching for his other hand.

He was quiet for a beat before dipping his chin in a nod. "I'm fine."

"I don't like your great-uncle," I said flatly.

"Join the club. He's a fucking asshole."

"Are you sure you're okay?" His hands were starting to warm in mine finally.

"I promise I'm okay."

"When should we go?"

"Now," he said, his lips curling up at one corner before stretching into a slow smile.

He stepped closer and bent low to press a hot kiss on the side of my neck, just beneath my ear. Goose-bumps broke out over my skin, and I shivered against him.

"Let's go. I don't actually want to make out in the

bathroom," I said, just as there was a loud knock on the door.

I felt the rush of his breath on my skin when he chuckled and dropped another hot kiss there. "Come on."

Chapter Twenty-Five

ARCHER

When we stepped outside, the air was icy, the cold striking against my cheeks. My body's thermostat was all out of whack. It always was on the heels of a panic attack or, in this case, an almost panic attack.

I tended to get cold first, and then once I started to warm, I got too hot. I took several deep gulps of the air, savoring its crispness and the scent of snow.

"It smells like it might snow," Phoebe offered as she walked beside me as if she could read my mind.

"It does. I love that smell."

She smiled up at me, the lights in the parking lot glittering on her hair. "Really?"

I squeezed her hand. "Yeah. It reminds me of Alaska and my childhood. It's hard to describe unless you know what it smells like."

She squeezed my hand again just as we reached my SUV. I'd been so out of it after seeing Clint that I forgot to use the remote start. "It'll take a minute to warm up." I opened the passenger door for her to climb in.

"We can handle it," she replied.

"Yeah, but you don't have a jacket."

She rolled her eyes. Moments later, we were driving away from the reception, and a delayed jolt of anger sliced through me. I couldn't fucking believe my uncle had shown up. But then I should have known. It was just the kind of thing he would do.

"Don't let him ruin it." Phoebe's voice reached me, and I slid my gaze sideways.

She was a mind reader, but I wasn't about to tell her that. "I'm not."

"What are you thinking about?"

The moment she asked that question, my mind conjured up the vision I'd been thinking about for fucking weeks now—Phoebe with her legs wrapped around my waist, sitting astride me. Because that's what I wanted. "You."

Her breath drew in sharply, her eyes widening slightly before she let out a startled laugh, the sound husky.

"Just being honest," I added with a shrug.

If anyone could make me forget, it was Phoebe. Because forgetting everything with her was the most real thing I could do.

The drive home wasn't too long. I pulled into the garage, and Phoebe said, "Home sweet home."

I tapped the button to turn off the engine before glancing her way. "It is home."

She blinked, her eyes glistening in the dim light.

"I'm so glad you're here," she whispered.

"You have no idea how glad I am that you're here."

I leaned over, palming her cheek as I brought my lips to hers. I meant for it to be a brief kiss. But the need I'd been barely holding in check kicked down the door, leaving my control in shambles. In a matter of seconds, our tongues were tangling, and I was devouring her mouth. She gasped into our kiss. It was only when I started to tug her across the console and my elbow hit the horn that we broke apart.

Her eyes went wide, and she burst out laughing. "You know, we're home. There's a bed inside and everything."

We were out of the SUV and through the door into the house in record time. I caught her hand in mine, reeling her to me, and was just about to fit my mouth over hers when she placed her palm on my chest. My heart kick-started into a fierce beat, recognizing her touch, knowing what she meant. This woman, my friend, who I'd never stopped loving. This was a new love for us, but the foundation underneath was unshakeable.

She stared up at me for a minute. "I know this started weird, but I love you."

My chest suddenly felt tight as emotion clenched around my heart. "It did, but it's for all the right reasons now. I love you," I whispered gruffly.

With her palm still pressed over my heart, it beat against her touch. She leaned up, pressing a kiss on the edge of my jaw. Then I was sliding my hand through her hair, and we were kissing again, stumbling through the entryway. We yanked at each other's clothes as we made our way to the bedroom, leaving a trail. The only time my uncle punctured my thoughts was when I remembered with relief that the house had a security system that automatically locked. Because he was just the man to try to show up here.

I kicked those thoughts away as Phoebe rolled her shoulders against the wall in the hallway, breaking away from my mouth. She gulped in air and giggled. "Oh, my god."

My hands rested on the wall beside her shoulders,

caging her between my arms. Phoebe's laughter faded as we stared at each other. I lifted a hand, reaching up to smooth loose locks of hair away from her cheeks. "Who did your hair?" I asked.

"Madison. Didn't she do a good job?"

I nodded. "It's beautiful. I want to take it down, but I'm not sure how."

Phoebe started giggling again. My shirt was open, and she was down to her bare breasts, which brushed against my skin with her laughter. "I'm not sure either."

She reached up, carefully running her fingers over the twist. A moment later, she had pulled out some pins, and they pinged on the floor as her hair fell around her shoulders.

My breath was hard to pull into my lungs, and my heart was giving sharp kicks against my ribs. "Fuck, you're gorgeous."

Pink crested on her cheeks, and she bit the corner of her lip. "Okay," she replied.

That shook a laugh loose. "Okay?"

Her lashes swept down before lifting again. "I'm not used to thinking of myself as gorgeous."

"You are, so accept the compliment."

When she took a deep breath, I felt her pebbled nipples and couldn't resist stepping back just enough so I could lean down. I sucked one into my mouth, and she let out a sharp gasp. And then I forgot everything else again as I mapped her body with my lips, teeth, and tongue.

We managed to stumble into the bedroom. The rest of our clothes were tossed on the floor, and I was pulling her over me as I sat on the foot of the bed. She stared at me, her eyes level with mine.

"Are we really doing this?" she rasped.

"Oh, we're doing this. We're already married."

Her smile was a little shy, and my heart thudded. "We are, huh? That's kind of crazy."

I shifted back on the bed, bringing her with me. It was messy, and she lost her balance, falling to the side at one point. I finally made it to the headboard, leaning against the pillows, and she shimmied upward. I felt the slick slide of her cleft over the underside of my cock and gritted my teeth.

She took a shaky breath and lifted her chin. "I thought it was silly that you wanted to wait. Maybe it was, but now it's a thing, and I'm anxious." Her lips twisted to the side, and uncertainty flickered in her eyes.

"It's only you and me." I lifted a hand, sliding it through her hair before it came to rest on the side of her neck. I gripped her hip with the other. "Come on now," I coaxed.

She rose, reaching between us. My cock notched at her entrance. We held still for a beat, and then she shifted, sliding down over me and bringing me into the silky glide of her core.

She was tight and so wet, I let out a ragged growl. She seated herself fully, wiggling her hips.

"Phoebe." Her name came out almost slurred. Dots danced around the edges of my vision as I stared at her. My gaze narrowed to her eyes.

She whispered my name before rising and sinking down again. Then we were rocking into each other in a slow rhythm. Each surge into her was deeper than the last. My release was already right there at the edge. I couldn't make this slow even though I wanted to. I was relieved that I could already feel her climax building. She was clenching and rippling around me, and her breath was coming in staccato gasps. Her body tightened before she arched deeply and released a keening cry, followed by my name.

I let go in deep, shuddering waves as my release slammed through me. She fell against me, warm and soft. I held her as I smiled, a sense of riotous joy thrumming through me.

Chapter Twenty-Six

PHOEBE

My eyes flew open in the darkness. I was still startled at awakening with Archer, my very own personal furnace, beside me. I smiled to myself. Last night had been so much more than I expected. It was only sex, but sex with Archer was something special. I got hot just thinking about it here in the darkness.

I cataloged the sensations in my body. I was a little sore. We'd ended up exploring each other more than once last night. Archer was never rough, but he also took me right to the edge, heightening every sensation. I took a deep breath, letting it out again, relaxation settling inside me. In spite of all of it, how this started almost as a lark when he proposed, none of that was what it was anymore. The fake was truly fake, and the real was truly real.

Archer rolled over on his back, murmuring something. He did that sometimes at night. We'd only been sleeping together for a week or so, yet I noticed he could be restless at night.

"Jake, no..." he muttered before lapsing into an almost sob.

Jake? He'd mentioned Jake's name three times now in his sleep. What was that about?

My mind spun to that awkward interaction with his great-uncle. An unsettled feeling rattled me again, interfering with my peace. Something about the look in his great-uncle's eyes I didn't like. It scared me and made me feel a little sick. It was the feeling I remembered way back in elementary school when we'd had the talk about safety, and I'd gone home and told my mom about it. She'd called it the uh-oh feeling and told me to trust it. I didn't trust that man, and I knew Archer didn't either. I wanted to understand why he had such an effect on Archer.

Archer made another sound, and I rolled over, curling against his side and placing my hand over his heart to discover it was racing. I moved my palm in a soothing circle. A moment later, he took a deep breath in his sleep, and I felt him come awake.

"Phoebe?" His voice was low and soft.

"Right here." I pressed a kiss on his collarbone, snuggling a little closer.

He shifted, his arm sliding around my shoulders. "Oh good, you're here."

"Where else would I be?" I asked lightly.

"I don't know. When I'm asleep, sometimes I get confused."

I almost commented about him talking in his sleep but decided against it. The long hours during darkness could be strange. Worry could chase its tail, and fears could loom larger than they actually were in the daylight hours.

"Nighttime is weird," I murmured, pressing another kiss on him, this time on his neck.

His hand was warm as it curled around my

shoulder and slid down my upper arm in a soothing pass. "I'm glad you're here."

"We're married," I pointed out.

He chuckled. "I know."

We fell quiet. With my hand circling lightly on his chest, his breathing evened out as he fell back asleep. I wondered just what secrets my brand-new husband and oldest friend held in his heart.

Chapter Twenty-Seven

PHOEBE

Archer turned off the water and handed me a towel. I almost dropped it. My body was languid, almost limp. We'd showered, and he'd fucked me up against the wall. It was glorious.

"Well, that's a way to start the morning," I managed dryly.

He chuckled and caught the towel just as it was about to slip free of my grip. He dried off, and I looked over at him, thinking if I wanted, I might be able to look at him for the rest of my life. A naked Archer was almost too much for the eyes—muscled and lean with that dusting of hair over his chest.

I admired the flex of his back muscles when he turned to hang up the towel and pulled on a pair of sweatpants. That was disappointing, as they covered up his ass. I never thought I'd have a thing for a guy's ass, but wow, Archer's was awesome. I could probably bounce a dime off it if I wanted. I used to think that was a ridiculous idea, but with his, well...

"Are you getting dressed?" he asked as he reached for his T-shirt and pulled it over his head.

I hadn't even dried off. I was dripping on the bath-mat. "Yes."

"I'll start the coffee," he called over his shoulder as he walked out of the bedroom.

After I dried off and pulled on my own pair of comfy leggings and a fluffy sweater, I stared at myself in the mirror. My hair was darker when it was wet. I rubbed the towel over it and ran a brush through it before fluffing it a little. My skin was flushed from the heat of the shower and Archer having his way with me.

God, this was weird. We were married. It was really *real* now. I was about to go have coffee with my new husband and step into a life I had never imagined having.

Bemused, I turned and made my way downstairs to the kitchen. The scent of coffee reached me, and I smiled when I saw Archer. He was standing by the stove, looking at something on his phone while he had his hand curled around a whisk in a stainless steel bowl beside a carton of eggs.

"What are you making?" I asked.

He glanced over. "I was going to make omelets, but I'm not sure I can pull it off."

"Omelets?"

"You love omelets," he said.

I stopped beside him, resting my hands on the counter and looking at his phone. He had pulled up some cooking website with a recipe for omelets. "Have we talked about omelets recently?"

He smiled sheepishly. "No, but you used to love the ones my mom made."

I thought my heart might fly straight out of my chest into the sky. "Wow, I forgot that."

His mom used to make omelets for us and make shapes with melted cheese on the top of them. I had loved them, but it'd been years since those memories filled my mind.

"We can just do scrambled eggs," I offered, aware Archer didn't cook too much.

"But I wanted to make them for you. It's our wedding morning breakfast."

"I think it's the day after," I teased, trying to keep light inside while emotion was swamping me.

He smiled, and I leaned up and brushed a kiss across his lips. "Scrambled eggs. I just want to have some coffee and relax. What are we doing? We haven't even discussed our honeymoon."

"You said you didn't want to talk about a honeymoon," Archer reminded me. "Let's go on a honeymoon."

"You're right. I didn't want to talk about it. We haven't had much time to plan. Plus, it's winter."

He smiled down at me. "I'm about to start making calls and whisk you away."

"The best time to leave Alaska isn't the middle of the winter. It's mud season. Don't you remember?"

Archer's eyes went wide before he chuckled. "You're right. It's a mess when the snow's melting."

"I'm off work for two weeks. Let's enjoy the house, and we'll plan a trip during mud season."

"Are you sure?" he pressed.

"I'm positive. Unless it's going to send the wrong message to your family about whether our marriage is real."

"Oh, sweetheart, our marriage is real." Archer set his phone on the counter and looped his arms around my waist.

"I know it's real, but your great-uncle's kind of an asshole, and he makes me nervous."

"Don't worry about him."

"But—"

Archer cut me off with a firm kiss. "Stop thinking about it. We're one-hundred-percent married, and it's consummated." He waggled his eyebrows at that.

I laughed as my cheeks got hot. "Let me help you with the eggs."

We made scrambled eggs with some feta and red peppers. I discovered that Archer's assistant worked magic. I had no idea how he pulled it off from a distance, but we were stocked up all the time.

"Is this how you normally live?" I asked as we were putting the dishes in the dishwasher.

"What do you mean?"

"I mean, does somebody order all your groceries and do all that all the time."

He shook his head. "No, just in a pinch. This was a pinch, sweetheart. I got my parents' house renovated, furnished, stocked, and we got married inside of two months. It was a pinch."

He crossed over to the coffee pot, refilling his mug and calling over, "Need a refill?"

"Yes, please."

He fetched my empty mug where it sat on the table and filled it before returning it to me. He leaned his hips against the island counter across from where I was standing by the sink.

"What now?" I asked. A giddy sense of joy was humming inside me.

"We embark on married life," he said with a slow smile.

"What are we going to do for the next two weeks?"

"Hang out. We never had trouble finding things to do when we were kids."

"Yeah, but we're not kids anymore."

"Let's go cross-country skiing."

"Oh!" I clapped my hands together. "That is perfect, but I don't have my skis."

"Yes, you do," he replied with a wink. "I called your parents. They told me you store them in their garage."

"And your assistant arranged to have them picked up?" I asked incredulously.

"Absolutely. He also arranged for my stuff to be delivered when I moved here."

I rolled my eyes. "You know my parents could have brought them over."

"I know, but I didn't want you to worry about it."

"I don't know what to do about this," I said, a thread of anxiety tangling inside the joy.

"Let's get ready and go for that ski," he prompted.

I decided to stop worrying about things I couldn't undo. I took a swallow of my coffee and pushed away from the counter. "All right, but I have to make sure I have my ski clothes."

"All of your clothes are here," he said as I strode past him.

I laughed when he swatted me on my bottom. I was walking down the hallway when I heard the sound of his phone chiming in the kitchen and then him answering. I could've sworn the air itself shifted in the hallway.

It felt as if an icy gust blew from the kitchen down toward me. I was maybe twenty feet away from Archer at this point, but I turned around and walked back into the kitchen. He was standing at the counter, gripping the phone tightly. His skin looked bleached, and his eyes were wide. I didn't know who was on the other end, but I could hear the muted sound of a voice.

Archer hadn't even noticed me when I reached his

side. His eyes swung to mine when I placed my hand on his back. The look in them was almost wild.

"Don't fucking call me," he said, hanging up quickly.

His breath was shallow, and he looked strange, not himself. "Archer, are you okay?"

He nodded jerkily, but he didn't move. He was gripping his mug so tightly I thought he might crack it. I reached for it and had to forcibly uncurl his fingers.

"Archer?" I prompted after I set his mug on the counter. "Who was that?" I pressed.

He stared at me, blinking rapidly. "My great-uncle," he said.

"Archer, you're not okay." My stomach churned with worry.

"I'm fine," he insisted.

I placed my hand over his heart to feel the beat of it racing. I took him by the hand and led him into the living room. He followed without a word, sitting down on the couch beside me. He muttered something, and I rubbed my hand on his back, wondering just what the hell was going on.

Within a few minutes, his breathing had returned to normal. His elbows were resting on his knees, and he lifted his hands, tunneling them roughly through his hair before he straightened.

"Sorry about that," he said.

"Archer, what's going on?"

"Nothing."

"This is not nothing. Please don't lie to me. What happened with him?"

His gaze dropped before he lifted his eyes to mine again. He straightened and leaned back into the couch cushions. "You remember what I told you about my cousin, Jake?"

"Yes," I replied carefully. He'd said Jake's name a few times when he was asleep.

"I think Jake had his reasons for blackout drinking. Clint used to beat Jake."

My hand clenched. "What?" I whispered. My stomach turned sickly. "What do you mean?"

"Just what I said. I don't know why, but he was the target for him. I found out, and Clint..." Archer paused, swallowing several times. "Hit me a few times."

"Oh, my god? Are you serious?"

His skin was still pale, although the color was returning. He looked almost ashamed.

"Archer. That's awful."

"Yeah, I know." His tone was level, flat, almost without emotion.

"Does anybody know?"

"You," was all he offered.

I threw a hand up in the air, and it whacked against the couch as it fell. "Did your parents know?"

"No. My cousin Rhys knows, but we don't talk about it."

"Nobody stopped him?"

Archer shrugged. "I don't know. All Jake wanted was to get the hell away from his granddad. Their father died. With so many kids, their grandparents, Clint and his late wife, often helped their mother, babysitting and so on. Jake and I had one conversation about it. We were visiting them, and my parents were out running errands. I heard voices in Clint's den and walked down the hallway. He hauled off and slapped Jake so hard, Jake stumbled. After that, he grabbed Jake and threw him against the wall."

"How many times did he hurt Jake and you? And who else?" I asked, fury burning like cold fire in my veins. I wanted to chase down his great-uncle and bring the wrath upon him.

Archer shrugged again. "Whenever I saw him, he would find a reason to rough me up. He never left marks, and I started to have panic attacks later."

"Archer. Oh my god," I breathed. "Why didn't you tell me?"

My throat ached, and I wanted to fix this.

My oldest friend, the man I'd fallen in love with, dipped his chin. "I don't know. It's weird, and I hate how it feels. I know I shouldn't be embarrassed, but I am. I'd appreciate it if you didn't tell anybody."

"Have you talked to a therapist? Maybe something can help and..."

"I know, Phoebe, I know." He reached for me, catching my hand in his and squeezing. Tears stung my eyes. "I handle them much better than I used to, but it's hard when I hear his voice."

"Do you have to talk to him?"

"He's part of my family, and he's a part of the business."

"But not the mine, right?"

Archer's smile was crooked, and it didn't reach his eyes. "No, not anymore."

"Does your grandmother know?"

"I don't know. My family isn't the chattiest. I love my parents, and they're good people, but we don't talk about stuff like this."

"How can I help?"

Chapter Twenty-Eight

ARCHER

How can I help?

Phoebe's question repeated in my thoughts. Her hair was drying in tousled waves around her shoulders, and her pretty eyes were so concerned. I couldn't even believe I had told her.

"I don't need you to do anything," I said, and I meant it.

My heart had kicked up again, but it wasn't panic. I seldom spoke about this. It was fucking stressful to talk about it to anyone. I felt as if I were crossing a boundary, kicking through a wall of steel that fell behind me. I still hadn't told her the whole story. Except for my great-uncle and my therapist and Jake, I wasn't sure if anyone else knew the whole of it. Rhys and I had only spoken of it once after Jake drank himself to death. Even then, our conversation had been vague.

Rhys knew Jake had been his grandfather's target, but to this day, I didn't know if he knew the whole truth. I felt as if I were carrying a heavy secret, a cold ball of darkness, weighing down a corner of my heart.

I didn't know what Clint would do. I never knew. I didn't fear for my safety even though I still had panic attacks. I just knew the worst thing about him, and I knew that was why he hated me.

"I'm sorry he showed up at the reception." I heard myself saying.

Phoebe squeezed my hand. "You don't need to apologize." She lifted her chin, and her eyes took on a gleam I knew well. It was the look she got when she would beat me in a race when we were kids. She would get the same look when she stood up against a bully who had been targeting a new kid in our class.

That look was why she was a hotshot firefighter. My wife was a fucking badass and didn't back down from a challenge.

"I'm even more than glad that we got married now," she said.

I chuckled. "Oh, yeah?"

"Hell, yeah. He doesn't call the shots anymore, and he has no power over you." She paused, cocking her head to the side and studying me. "I think you should tell your grandmother."

"Phoebe—" I began.

"Listen to me," she pressed. "Secrets make things worse."

I swallowed and took a breath. "It's long over, and Jake is dead. I'm fine. I'm not afraid of him anymore."

"You have panic attacks!" she yelped.

"Fair enough, but I'm rational. Because I did see a therapist, I know that's just my unconscious nervous system reacting. She told me his voice was a trigger. It flicks a switch and turns off my thinking brain." I tapped my forehead. "That's the frontal lobe."

"I know," she said dryly.

"Maybe someday I'll talk to my grandmother about

it. Rhys knows. I don't think it's a secret in the family. It's just not something I want to talk about. Who will it help anyway?" I knew I was glossing this over, but I meant what I said. "Jake is dead. Clint's not going to assault me now. He's fucking old."

"How old is he?"

"He's like, seventy or so. He's got arthritis."

"Yeah but—"

"Phoebe, you asked what you could do. I will talk to you about it, but please don't try to make me do anything about this."

"Okay," she whispered.

Her lips twisted to the side, and she leaned over, sliding her arms around my waist. It was a little awkward on the couch. She rested her palm over my heart, circling it just like she had last night. She'd put me back to sleep. I never remembered those dreams, but I usually woke up feeling unsettled and anxious and thinking I was dreaming about Jake even though I couldn't remember the details.

"You still want to ski?" I asked.

She straightened, peering up at me and studying me. "Do you want to? It's not just my day," she said.

"I know. I'd like to ski." She smiled slightly. "I haven't been cross-country skiing since I was here. I used to love it. It'd be a great way to take my mind off that stupid phone call."

"Why does he even call you?"

"To be an asshole. He's not pleased I'm taking over this entire branch of the company."

"Why is it that way? I'm honestly curious."

"When my grandparents started the business, it was just a vineyard, but they invested in real estate and mineral rights in areas all over Alaska, and things got big. My grandfather gave his brother a job but no power in the company. Long story short, Clint was a placeholder until I got married. He's just always had it out for me, I think, because of what I know."

Phoebe muttered something under her breath.

"What?"

She glanced up. "I'm just mad. He's an asshole."

"Tell me something I don't know," I said dryly. "It's all about control with him."

"Will you at least call Rhys and make sure he's not going to muck stuff up while you're taking the next two weeks off?" she asked.

"Already taken care of. Now, let's go skiing."

I really needed to snap out of this mood. I shifted and stood, catching her hand in mine as her arms slid away from me.

An hour or so later, I leaned my head back and let out a whoop, the sound echoing in the crisp, cold air. Phoebe laughed, and I looked over at her. Her cheeks were bright pink, and her breath puffed in the air.

The sky was a sharp blue. It was a perfect day for cross-country skiing. We had just come through some trees out into an open valley.

Phoebe lifted her ski pole, pointing at a groomed trail. "You remember that?"

I held up my own ski pole, twirling it in the air. "I think so."

"It's a fun downhill, but there's a jump at the bottom because we have to cross a creek. You up for that? Or, has it been too long?"

"I might not have been cross-country skiing lately, but I've kept up on my downhill skiing." Race you?"

Phoebe bit her bottom lip. "Of course. I'll beat you."

I watched as she pushed off. I knew she might beat me, but I wasn't going to make it that easy. I bent low as I pushed off my own poles. We flew down the hill, curled tightly with our ski poles tucked to our sides. She started to gain a little speed on me, and I watched as she reached the bottom of the hill, lifting her legs just in time to fly over the narrow creek. I followed suit, landing maybe a second behind her.

We were laughing as we slowed. When I stopped as close as I could to her, she caught my eyes. She was breathing hard, and her smile was wide. Pure joy gusted through me like a fresh breeze.

"This is awesome. I'm glad you're back, Archer."

It wasn't easy. In fact, the angle was downright awkward when I leaned sideways on my skis to kiss her. Her lips were warm, a contrast to the icy cold air.

"Any more hills on the way home?" I asked when I straightened.

She shook her head. This day was perfect, and I forgot everything about this morning.

Chapter Twenty-Nine

ARCHER

"What the hell?" I adjusted my earbud.

Rhys's sigh filtered through the line. "I know. My granddad's a fucking ass. He's flipping out, but it's already a done deal. Our attorneys looked it over. The will is locked tight. He can't contest it."

I paused, collecting my thoughts. "You know what? I'm going to shut down that office."

"The building?" my cousin asked.

"Yep. I don't trust his staff."

"Nobody likes him."

"Look, we can reassign them, but this prevents his bullshit. I'm going to shut him out electronically this morning."

I felt torn about Phoebe's suggestion that I talk to my grandmother about him. Clint was her brother in law, but maybe that was the only way to put a stop to this. The whole thing was wearying.

Rhys chuckled. "I think that's your best move. Do you want my help relocating the staff?"

"Let's figure out who we plan to keep and who we can't trust. I hate firing people."

I could feel my cousin's eye roll through the phone line. "Yeah, it sucks. Honestly, from what I know, the two main ones to worry about are his assistant and the VP."

"Seriously? His assistant has always been nice to me."

"Yeah, because he likes to get all the gossip. He thinks he's good at it, but he's not."

"Okay, so they're both gone. Anyone else?"

"I'll check with my assistant. She usually knows the scoop. Let's have the meeting together with the VP."

"I don't mind handling it," I said.

"I thought you said you hated firing people."

"Well, I don't mind firing people for a reason. If he's undermining others, that's a good reason. Plus, I know he's comfortable financially. It's when I worry about people's income that I get stressed, even if they deserve to be fired."

"You need to work on your ruthless streak," my cousin teased.

This time, I rolled my eyes. "I'll get right on that, dude. You're so fucking ruthless."

We burst out laughing.

An hour later, I had electronically locked Clint, his VP, and his assistant out of everything, including the buildings. Although I could have had someone do it for me, plunking around on the back end of computer programs was personally relaxing for me. I loved finding solutions. Not that I needed a solution in this case, but I didn't want there to be any missteps. I knew if I did it, there wouldn't be.

I glanced at the clock. It read 11:30 a.m. I expected a phone call within the hour, if not sooner. As I predicted, he called within forty-five minutes. My phone vibrated on my desk. I stared at it, watching his name flash on the screen. For the first time in years, maybe since the day I'd started carrying his secret, I didn't experience a jolt of fear. Oh, that old panic was there, hovering under the surface, but he no longer had the power to influence me or my life, not directly at least.

I contemplated ignoring his call, but I was only delaying the inevitable. I put my earbuds in and tapped the call button. "Hello."

"What the fuck, Archer?" he opened with.

"What's up?" I asked, keeping my tone light.

"You locked me out of all the systems, and my VP and assistant."

"I did. You're fired, effectively relieved of all your duties. HR is handling the details for it."

"I need access to things. You need my help with the transition."

"No, I don't. I don't trust you."

The phone went silent. If it was possible to feel anger from two-thousand-plus miles away where he was in Seattle, I could feel it. Lord knows how many cell towers relayed the signal. The line was silent, heavy, and dark.

"You fucking prick. You've always just been a little shit," he muttered.

"It is what it is. We've already reviewed it with the attorneys. You can't contest the will, you know it, and I don't want to work with you, so I'm not going to."

"I'm going to talk to—"

Even though my pulse was racing and my throat felt tight, I managed to cling to my anger. "Who are you going to talk to? Rhys already knows what I'm doing."

"I'm going to talk to your grandmother."

"And what is she going to do? There's nothing you

can fucking do. You manipulated your way in and bullied my dad as much as you could, but I don't want any part of this. I know you're not going to fuck with me," I said flatly.

"You don't know what you saw that day." I was instantly shocked he spoke aloud about that moment.

"Oh, I know exactly what I saw."

This was the first time he'd ever even alluded to that situation. It had always hung in the air between us. My heart was pounding in a sickly beat, and my gut was churning.

"Fuck you." The line went dead.

I checked the phone to make sure the call was officially off. I even powered it down. That was a lingering paranoia I had with him. There were too many mistakes as far as technology was concerned. I didn't want to accidentally leave a call line open with him. That was a habit I'd learned he used at the office, so he could listen in on conversations.

Leaving my phone off, I stood from my desk and paced in a restless circle. I shook my arms to discharge the panic churning in my chest. My fingertips were tingling, and I felt that static cold rolling through me.

"Archer."

Phoebe's voice reached me from the door. When I turned and met her eyes, I knew I couldn't mask what was going on,

"What's wrong?" She was at my side in seconds, reaching for my hands. "Oh my god, your hands are freezing. Archer, what happened?"

I tried to speak, but I couldn't. Closing my eyes, I took a deep breath. Simply trying to stand still was overwhelming me, so I slipped my hands free of hers and began pacing back and forth again.

I was relieved she stayed quiet. My heartbeat

began to slow, and I finally turned to face her. "I fired Clint, so he called."

"I hate him." The fierce protectiveness in her voice sent warmth through me. Her presence radiated around me, chasing away the cold, panicky fear that was such a reflex around him. The therapist I'd seen in Seattle called it my trauma brain. When it got triggered, my ability to be rational was limited and not usually available to me. My trauma brain was driving the car, so to speak, and had a firm grip on the steering wheel.

"Do you have to talk to him again?" she pressed.

I shook my head, managing to actually smile a little as I felt my frontal lobe click back online. "We shut him out electronically, so he can't even get in the offices because he needs his code to work."

Phoebe reached for my hands. This time, I didn't pull away. She stepped closer and wrapped her arms around my waist, pressing her cheek against my chest over my heart. "I want to beat him up."

When she leaned back and peered up at me, her eyes were so earnest, I couldn't help but laugh even though it was tinged with bitterness. "I do too, but it won't change what happened."

"I know, but he deserves it." He did, and not just for what she knew. The whole truth was still my secret. "Are you going to work tonight?" she asked.

I shook my head.

"Good. You know what I think we should do?"

"Uh, no?"

"We should go to Wildlands. You can hang out with your old friends and forget all this. What do you think?"

"Let's do it. I don't need to work this evening, and I want to spend time with you and just be here."

Her smile felt like a ray of sun shining directly into my heart. "First, let's shower."

"Shower?"

"Yeah, showers are grounding. It'll snap you out of that shitty conversation."

Bemused, I shrugged.

"You've got that whole like rainwater system set up here. We're not even wasting water," she offered with a grin.

I let her lead me into the shower. She swatted me away when I tried to get a little frisky, telling me now wasn't the time.

"Later," I said as we were toweling off.

Chapter Thirty

PHOEBE

"You did not." Susannah leaned across the table, her brows rising as she looked at Madison.

Madison pursed her lips and shrugged. "I absolutely did." Susannah leaned back, letting her breath out in a huff before glancing at Paisley and me. We were the only three female hotshots in Willow Brook. Susannah had just shared her morning moose encounter where she had chased off two moose.

"You've got more nerve than any of us." Graham chuckled beside Madison.

"I know, right? I'm definitely on the losing end of any argument. I can vouch she chased those moose off. Saw it myself," Ward chimed in.

Archer laughed softly beside me, and I glanced at him. "What?" I asked, my voice low, just for him to hear.

"It's just funny seeing everybody all grown up. Everybody's the same yet different. You are too." His arm was resting across my shoulders, and he squeezed his fingers lightly over my upper arm.

I loved the feeling of having Archer back here in

my world. I was still adjusting to the fact that he was this hot, sexy man. Well, that and the fact we were married. Minor detail. And, sweet Jesus, he knew how to make me fly in bed.

"How is it?" Graham asked, addressing his question to Archer.

"How's what?" Archer countered.

"Married life, being back in Willow Brook, running a multibillion-dollar company. You know, all that." Graham circled his hand in the air.

Archer grinned. "Shall I answer in order?"

"Sure," Graham replied easily.

"Being married is great. I think it's the best decision I've ever made." He shifted his arm, his palm resting just between my shoulder blades. He squeezed his fingers lightly at the base of my neck, sending a shiver chasing down my spine. "And it's good to be back in Willow Brook. Maybe I've been away longer than I lived here, but it feels like home. It's where I grew up, you know?"

"I never left, so I don't know, but I think some other people would agree," Graham commented.

"As far as the company, I've been working there since I graduated from college, so it's not that new. The difference now is I'm running an entire division."

"I think that'll be good," Maisie interjected. She was sitting across from us and leaned forward with a glint in her eyes. "What are you going to do about the mine?"

"I'm closing it," Archer said matter-of-factly.

Maisie squealed and clapped her hands. "You are?"

"That's the plan."

"Oh wow, is this public information, or is it a secret?" She actually looked around as though she needed to worry about who might overhear.

Beck rolled his eyes beside her before taking a long drag of his beer. "I don't think Archer would tell you if it was a secret."

Maisie cast him a glare. "If he told me it was private information, I would *not* tell anyone."

Archer grinned. "It's not. We haven't announced it, but it's not a secret."

"Will it affect the bottom line?" Madison asked.

I could practically see the little ticker clicking in her brain. Madison was an actuary, and big numbers were her thing.

"Probably," Archer replied. "But I already have contingency plans in place. I actually meant to reach out to you about that."

"About what?" Madison prompted.

"Phoebe told me you're an actuary. Do you consult?"

"Of course." Madison straightened and took on what I considered to be her professional look, although she always looked professional. "Phoebe has my number. You can call anytime. I'd say we could chat tonight, but I've had two glasses of wine." Graham leaned over, pressing a kiss on her cheek.

"I'll be in touch sooner rather than later," Archer replied.

"Aren't you on your honeymoon?" Paisley chimed in.

I shrugged. "Sort of, but not really. We decided just to take the two weeks here and plan a trip later."

Archer chimed in, "We're going somewhere warm during mud season."

"Mud season is absolutely the best time to go on vacation," Maisie commented. "The weather is shitty, and by then, you're impatient for winter to be over.

Are you actually staying through the rest of the winter?"

"That's the plan. I like winter, and I missed Willow Brook." He squeezed lightly on my neck again. I realized I was going to have to give him some instructions. He was getting me all hot and bothered, and we were in a public place.

"Hey, Archer," a familiar voice said.

I glanced over to see Chase approaching the table. Archer twisted in his chair, a grin breaking across his face as he stood from the table. "Hey, man."

Chase stopped in front of him, pulling him into a back-slapping hug before stepping back. "Sorry I missed the wedding."

"No worries. Phoebe told me you were out of town."

I smiled up at Chase. "I knew you would have wanted to be there."

Chase grinned. "I did. I've been gone for a few weeks, and you don't waste time. I heard you've redone your parents' old place and you're married. It's fucking crazy."

Madison scooted her chair over. She snagged an empty chair from a nearby table, pulling it beside her. "Sit."

Chase chuckled. "Thanks." He sat between her and Archer, resting his elbows on the table. Chase was on our firefighter crew, and he'd been out of town for some kind of family matter. Chase and Archer had been friends when we were kids. He was an old friend of mine as well, and now we worked together. He felt like a brother to me. It still shocked me that Archer didn't feel like a brother.

As soon as Archer sat down again, he curled his

arm across my shoulders. "How've you been?" he asked Chase.

"Pretty good," Chase said with a shrug.

Now wasn't the time, but I sensed something was going on with Chase. Objectively speaking, he was very handsome. He was a bit of a flirt but also kind of quiet. I eyed him with a consideration I never had before. I was still so startled by my reaction to Archer that I found myself measuring up every old guy friend I had. I couldn't even summon the remotest attraction for Chase. Yet the second I looked at Archer, my belly did a little flip. I kept thinking my reaction would start to fade. If anything, it was getting worse.

Chase and Archer caught up on life, and as I sat there with my friends and Archer, a sense of peace settled inside. It was as if a breeze had blown through me. The sense of ease that came with our friendship slipped into the space around us, mingling with my new emotions, which were intense and sometimes overwhelming. At one point, he glanced down, waggling his eyebrows when he asked if I wanted another glass of wine, and a laugh bubbled up.

"What's so funny?" he asked.

"You used to do that all the time," I replied.

"I definitely didn't use to ask you if you wanted a glass of wine when we were kids," he replied dryly.

Chase chuckled. "Definitely not."

"No, the eyebrow thing." I gestured, lifting my fingers up and down and mimicking the motion of his eyebrows.

"I did?" Archer looked surprised.

"Yes!"

He shrugged. "Okay, whatever. My question still stands."

"Sure. Are you driving?" I asked.

"I drove us here, didn't I? I'm not having more than this beer," he said, spinning his empty beer bottle between his fingers. He glanced at his watch. "I just finished it, so we won't leave for an hour."

"I'll take another glass of wine then." At that moment. I happened to glance toward Chase, whose attention had been drawn away from the table. "Girlfriend?" I asked.

Chase glanced back at me, his eyes going wide. "Uh, no."

"Well, you're looking pretty hard," I teased. He rolled his eyes. "Do you know her?"

"Her name's Hallie. That's all I know," Chase replied.

Archer eyed him. "I should have known you'd turn out to be a first name kind of guy."

"What does that mean?" Chase pressed.

"Dude, I may have moved away before high school, but you were a flirt even then. Every week, you had a new girl you were 'going with,'" Archer replied, complete with air quotes.

Chase shrugged. "I'm not ready to get serious. Maybe you're married and settling down, but I don't think that's for me."

"No? Tell me why not," Archer pressed. "I don't know anybody who thinks playing the field is a great plan for long term."

Chase cast a baleful look around the table. "Right. Practically everybody here is paired up except for me. No, I just..." He shifted his shoulders, and, in a rare moment, he looked uncertain.

I experienced a stab of sympathy for him. Chase was a good guy, but life hadn't always been smooth for him. "It's just not for me. That's all," he said lightly, brushing off Archer's question. Chase excused himself not much later, commenting he had someone to meet.

After that, I noticed him with his elbows resting on the bar. He was smiling down at Hallie, who definitely wasn't from Willow Brook.

As we were driving home, I asked Archer, "So how did it feel to see everyone?"

Archer cast me a thoughtful look. "I meant it when I said Willow Brook always felt like home."

"Why did no one else come to manage the mine after you all moved away?" I asked.

"My parents transferred to the home offices in Fireweed Harbor. Clint was appointed to handle this division, but he didn't want to move here. With technology and such, it's not difficult to handle issues remotely."

"Is this a conversation we should have?" I asked, a sense of uncertainty spinning in my chest.

"What do you mean?"

"Well, you're here now, but do you want to live here?"

"I do," he said firmly. "I'll need to travel some, but you can come with me if you want, or we can figure something else out. You don't have to work, you know."

"You mean be a firefighter?"

"I'm not saying you need to stop. I'm just saying, financially speaking, you don't need to work."

It was not that this hadn't crossed my mind. Archer had mentioned it before, but I'd been keeping it at bay.

As if he sensed my anxiety, he added, "Let's just play it by ear and not stress out about it now."

I took a quick breath. "Okay."

"You're stressing, aren't you?" he asked, his eyes

shifting to mine quickly before he looked back at the road.

"This is weird. We didn't plan any of this."

"I don't think it's any weirder than most of the world. We have a lot more of a foundation than many marriages. Some people do the whole thing—yearlong engagement, huge wedding, the whole thing—then it still falls apart. We were best friends when we were kids. Even though we haven't seen each other in a long time, I feel like I know you better than I know most anybody."

He reached over, his hand landing just at the base of my neck. He squeezed lightly, a gesture that was becoming familiar. I took another quick breath. "You're right. It's just different, and you're really rich. I know your parents had money, obviously, but it's not something I thought about when we were little."

"And, it's not something you need to think about now. It doesn't change me or us."

"Yeah, but you just told me I didn't have to have a job. I *need* to have a job. Maybe not financially, but I can't imagine not doing something productive. How are you going to feel when I go out to fight fires? We haven't talked about this," I blurted out.

Considering that our entire relationship had taken place during the winter when things were the quietest for hotshot crews, Archer hadn't faced me leaving for weeks at a time.

"Phoebe, please don't freak out."

He turned onto the road where we lived. I'd come to visit this house so many times when we were kids, and now I shared it with him. He slowed, coming to a stop right in the middle of the road.

"What are you doing?" I yelped.

He turned, facing me. "Phoebe, there's no traffic. It's fine. Look at me."

I stared into his eyes, and the whirling anxiety that had started to spin in my chest slowed. "Just one day at a time, okay? Just give me that. I know you're a firefighter. I can deal. Hell, I can even plan any travel I have to do around when you go out in the backcountry. It'll be fine."

"But what about if we get a pet, or we have kids?"

"Well, we'd have to figure that out anyway. Susannah is a firefighter, and she and Ward have a kid." He was all practical and unruffled.

Just looking into his eyes calmed me. My anxiety notched down another level with every second, and I finally took a slow breath. "You're right. I don't need to freak out."

He leaned over, pressing a quick and fierce kiss on my lips just as headlights flickered behind us. "Let's go home."

Chapter Thirty-One

PHOEBE

Three weeks later

I stepped through the doorway to my parents' house, calling, "Hey Mom, hey Dad!"

My mother called from the kitchen, "Hey, Phoebe! Come on back here. I'm in the kitchen."

After toeing off my boots, I hung my jacket by the door, then leaned down to greet my parents' elderly dog, Grayson, who was very gray now. "Hey, bud." He nudged my knees with his nose and walked slowly at my side as we made our way into the kitchen.

My mother was checking the oven and turned to press a kiss on my cheek when I stopped at her side. "Is Archer coming tonight?" she asked.

"No, I told you, he had some work meetings to deal with." Archer was coming back late this evening from a meeting in Anchorage.

"At night?"

"Yes, Mom. They handle stuff all over the place. Anyway, where's Dad?"

"Upstairs in his study. He'll be down in a few."

"Can I do anything?" I asked.

"Nope. The lasagna will be out in just a few minutes, and the salad is ready. Have a seat."

My parents' kitchen was one of my favorite places to be. I'd spent countless hours here during my childhood. The table by the windows offered a gorgeous view, and tonight's sunset was splashy with swirls of pink, lavender, and fading to silver-gold.

I rested my elbows on the table and took a sip of the water my mother had already set in front of me. "So how are things, Mom?"

"Oh, you know, busy. Always. Tell me, how is married life?"

"It's good." I felt the heat rise in my cheeks because the reasons it was great—beyond the fact that Archer was my best friend again—weren't things I wanted to share with my mother. She adjusted the timer on the oven before walking over to sit down across from me.

"I still feel like it was fate," she commented.

"What?"

"You and Archer."

"Mmm," I offered vaguely.

I wasn't going to fess up to her how it all started. She didn't need to know that. Just then, my father walked into the kitchen. He looked distracted, but that wasn't a surprise. He had the look of a distracted scientist most of the time. My parents ended up in Alaska when he took a job with the federal government as a biologist, and he loved it.

"Are you counting fish, Dad?" I called over.

His smile was quick. "Always." He fetched a beer from the refrigerator. "Do you need some wine?" he asked my mother.

She shook her head. "Not tonight."

A moment later, he was sitting beside my mother. We chatted about the usual—the weather, day-to-day stuff, and work.

I sensed my father was more than his usual version of distracted. He seemed stressed. My mother had gotten up to get the lasagna out of the oven, and I asked, "Is everything okay, Dad?"

He was quiet for a beat before he replied, "I don't know."

My mother—because she had bat ears as I'd dubbed them when I was a kid—turned quickly as she walked over with the casserole held atop an oven mitt. "What is going on? You've been distracted since this morning."

My father took a quick breath. "Well, I don't know actually. Do you recall I was on the board at Archer's company years back?"

"What do you mean?" I asked.

"Back when his parents ran it, I was on the board. It was a perfunctory duty, frankly. Anyway, I had an email. I expected some communication with the changeover to Archer. But this wasn't that." He paused, his eyes dipping down.

"What is it, Dad?" I couldn't have said why, but my gut pinged uncomfortably.

My mother set the lasagna down on the table before plunking down in the chair beside him.

"Archer's great-uncle is threatening to call out that loan," he added.

"What loan, Dad?" I asked, genuinely confused. Of course, that gut feeling intensified at the mention of Archer's great-uncle.

My father sighed. "I made some bad investments,

and we were in a bind. At the time, I made a bad decision."

"What do you mean?"

"I took out a balloon mortgage through the company. I thought I could make things up in time. I've been negotiating the loan, but Clint is demanding the balloon payment. I just don't have the money."

"I'll talk to Archer," I said immediately.

My father's eyes narrowed. "You will not."

"Don't be ridiculous, and don't be stubborn about this," I protested.

"Well, I have some pride. I don't feel comfortable asking my new son-in-law, who I like and respect, for money. I still remember him as the little boy who smeared blue paint all over the walls in the garage."

"It wasn't just him," I returned.

My mother rolled her eyes, and I smiled, thinking of that day we'd come across cans of paint and had some fun with it. My smile disappeared quickly.

"What kind of payment are we talking about? I asked.

"Fifty thousand dollars," my father said, his tone dry as chalk.

"But what does this have to do with the board?"

"Because of my connections there, I asked for some advice. Clint set up the loan through some option they offer to employees."

"Clint is bad news," I said.

"Well, he's always been nice to me."

All the while, my mother was quiet. I stole a glance at her to see the worry in her eyes as she traced her fingers over the nubbled surface of an oven mitt.

"But Dad..." I hesitated because I didn't feel comfortable sharing what I knew about Archer's great-uncle. I hewed as closely to the truth as I could without revealing any of that. "Archer does not trust him, and I can't help but wonder if him doing this now has something to do with me marrying Archer. Clint's really upset about losing control of this division. Dad, please let me ask him. I won't ask him for the money, but let me ask him what's going on. I'm sure he can help sort it out."

My father had been quietly drumming his fingertips on the table, a sure sign he was nervous. He was a fidgety man and fiddled more when he was nervous. "I don't mind you asking him, but I am not asking for money. I want to make that clear."

"I understand that. I'll talk to him tonight."

My father nodded, the littlest bit of relief crossing his face. "I'd appreciate it if we could figure this out. I've been making the payments regularly."

"Dad, you're not a rich man. You're a biologist."

My father shrugged, and my mother squeezed his hand before announcing we needed to put a pause on this conversation. "We can't solve it now, so let's not dwell."

I couldn't help but notice my father didn't dig into his dinner with his usual gusto. I left that night, resolved to talk to Archer as soon as he got home.

Chapter Thirty-Two

ARCHER

I turned into my driveway, my weariness lifting when I saw the lights from the house glowing through the darkness. Phoebe's car was parked inside the garage when I pulled in. With everything going on, I was in the midst of major restructuring with the local offices in Anchorage. That meant long days. I was trying to only go to Anchorage two or three days a week, so I wasn't gone too much.

It felt so good to come home to her. Not that I had any doubts, but every single day when I drove home tired from these meetings, the second I turned into our driveway—I loved thinking of it as *our* driveway—I felt a little lighter. She always made sure there was something to eat even though I told her she didn't have to.

A moment later, I was entering the kitchen. Phoebe was sitting at the counter, a glass of wine in hand, and her feet hooked around the legs of a stool. She smiled over at me. "Hey."

As soon as I had my shoes off and coat hung, I

crossed over to her, leaning down to give her a lingering kiss. "Hey, how was your day?"

"All right. Yours?"

"Busy." I glanced around the kitchen. "It smells good, but I don't see what you made."

She smiled. "My mom made an extra pan of lasagna for you. It's in the oven."

"Oh, wow, seriously? I remember your mom's lasagna. It's amazing."

"It's my dad's favorite, so she's constantly perfecting it. Do you want a beer or some wine?" Phoebe asked.

She stood and rounded the island to fetch a bowl from the cabinet before pulling the lasagna out of the oven.

"I can get my own beer, you know," I said as I opened the fridge and pulled one out.

A few minutes later, I moaned after another bite. "This is so good," I said flatly after I finished chewing.

Phoebe smiled over at me. "I know."

I sensed she was waiting for something. I took another bite before asking, "What's up? You look worried."

"Finish eating." Her voice was a little too bright, and I knew she was concerned about something.

"I can eat and listen." I took another bite and circled my free hand in the air.

Her shoulders rose as she took a deep breath. After that, she sipped her wine. "Okay, here's the situation. Apparently, my father used to be on the board at your family's company." I nodded. "And he made some bad investments years ago. He needed to refinance my parents' house. I don't know exactly why, but he did some kind of direct financing loan program through the company with your uncle."

"What? There's no loan program through the company."

"Well, my father says there is, or I guess there was. There's a balloon payment coming due, and he got an email from your great-uncle saying that if he doesn't make the balloon payment, Clint is going to repossess their home."

I had just taken another bite and swallowed quickly before leaning back. "No."

"What do you mean, no? My dad is really embarrassed for me to even say anything to you about it."

"I will pay off your parents' house if this is a real thing. But I don't think it is."

"My dad won't let you do that," Phoebe said, shaking her head.

"Sweetheart, we're going to figure this out. It's my uncle, so I'm guessing it's some kind of bullshit. He's probably trying to get to me through you by extension of your parents."

She chewed on her bottom lip before she let out a shaky sigh. "We can figure this out, right?"

"Absolutely. I'm not going to call Clint because that'll tip him off. No matter what, I won't let him manipulate your dad like this. I promise."

Phoebe stood from her stool and was around the counter in a flash, throwing her arms around me. "Thank you, thank you!" she exclaimed. "I told them you would figure it out."

"I will."

She pressed an enthusiastic kiss on my cheek before dropping her arms and sitting down across from me again. "Okay, sorry. I wanted you to be done eating before I told you. Are you stressed out?"

"I'm pissed about the situation, but this is a manageable thing. If he was doing something off the books with the company, that's not okay. We don't have a loan program like that. I would know by now."

It didn't ruin my appetite because it was a solvable problem. When I lay in bed later that night, though, my mind turned over the situation. It rankled me that he was going after Phoebe's parents to get to me.

The following evening after a call with Rhys, I decided my best option was to fly to Seattle. I didn't want to leave at all. I was going to miss Phoebe, even if it was only for a few days.

"I don't want to go," I said honestly. We were in the kitchen again, our usual place to eat together.

Her big blue eyes held mine, a flush cresting high on her cheeks. "I don't want you to go." She paused and finished the last swallow of her wine. "This is weird for me."

"What's weird?"

She waved her hand in the air. "All of this. I didn't expect to fall in love with you."

My heart thumped against my ribs. "Is it all that surprising?"

She looked down at her empty wine glass, tracing her fingertip around the base before lifting her eyes to mine again. "I guess not." Her gaze arced around the kitchen. "This is your old kitchen."

"Uh, yeah." I wasn't sure where she was going with this.

"It's fancy now, and you're rich."

I reached for her hand, where she was starting to nervously trace the edge of the counter.

"Phoebe. You were my best friend before, and I never forgot you. We still have that."

"I think it's a little different, Archer." Her voice rose several octaves at the end as the flush on her cheeks deepened.

"Well, yeah. Is that so bad?" I pressed.

Her hair swung when she shook her head swiftly. "I'm just— Now, you're flying away, and I'm going to miss you."

"I promise I'm only going to be gone as long as I need to be to deal with this."

"What do you think is going on?"

"I think Clint probably made a personal loan to your parents and made it seem like it was a company thing when it really wasn't. He didn't have the money to loan, though, so that means he embezzled the money from the company. Have your parents heard from him again?"

"Just one more email from him reminding them that they need to deal with it soon," she said, her words coming out in a rush followed by a shaky sigh.

"Were you planning to tell me that?" I asked gently.

Phoebe shrugged. "I didn't want to talk about it. My parents are pretty uncomfortable about it."

"They shouldn't be. My uncle did something illegal, and it's not okay. We're going to fix it."

Phoebe took a quick breath, then squeezed my hand. "Thank you."

"I'm going to miss you too."

"Do you know how long you'll be gone?"

"I'm hoping only a few days. I think I should plan on a week to be on the safe side."

"A whole week?"

She looked as dismayed as I felt. "Yes, but I'm hoping I can resolve it more quickly than that."

She let out a short sigh and squeezed my hand again. "Fine. I don't like it."

"You can come with me," I offered.

"No, I don't want to do that. I want to be here for

my parents because they're kind of freaking out. My dad's looking at his retirement funds and figuring out how much money he can pull out and things like that."

I nodded. Even though I wanted her with me for the sake of her presence, I didn't want her with me for this. I knew I was going to be dealing with Clint more than once. I suspected my panic was going to rise like a high tide. I'd already texted the therapist I'd seen in Seattle before, planning to check in with her while I was there.

"Should I drive you to the airport?"

"I don't need—" I began.

"I want to," she pressed. "Or are you taking a private plane?"

I chuckled. "No, I'm not. That's really bad for the environment. Flying, in general, is bad enough."

Phoebe giggled. "It is. I'll drive you there tomorrow."

"My flight leaves at four in the morning."

"Perfect. It'll be an adventure."

"Yeah. I love getting up that early. It feels like the rest of the world is asleep."

I gave her hand a light tug. "Come here," I murmured, gratified when she stood and immediately rounded the counter.

Her hands rested on my knees as I pulled her closer. "We'll straighten this out, and then I'll be back."

She nodded as her forehead fell to mine. "Promise?" Her lips moved against mine.

"Of course."

Then we were kissing, and I forgot about everything but Phoebe.

Chapter Thirty-Three

ARCHER

"I told you this was sketchy," I said to my cousin.

Rhys was pacing in front of the windows. "I knew my granddad was an asshole. I honestly never thought he would do this."

"Really? Not much surprises me with him."

My cousin stopped pacing and stuffed his hands in his pockets as he studied me. My hips were resting against the edge of his desk, and my arms were crossed.

"He moved some money from one dedicated retirement account for the company where we kept investment funds into his own personal account and then made loans. Phoebe's parents have been paying him directly. Except it goes into a bank, so they think it's a company loan. What do you want to do about it?"

Rhys leaned his head back as he stared at the ceiling for a moment before he commenced pacing back and forth in front of the windows. "I don't fucking know."

"We can definitely charge him, but I don't know how you feel about that." That was what I wanted to do, but I didn't want to press my cousin too hard yet.

He took a breath. For the first time, I sensed his trepidation. "I don't fucking know," he repeated.

"What do you want to do?" I asked again.

He stopped pacing. "I think we should charge him. It's an easy case. He's gotten away with a lot. He might as well face the consequences for something."

"I think we need to talk to Gram first."

Rhys stared at me for several beats, surprising me when he asked, "What do you know that I don't?"

"About what?" My stomach turned over, and I instantly felt sick as that staticky panic filled my chest. I wasn't going to have a panic attack, but I knew what my cousin was asking.

"About my grandfather. Do you know what happened with my brother?"

Oh, fuck. This was getting real, more real than I ever imagined. It was one thing for my cousin to know my uncle had been physically abusive to his brother. But I was pretty sure Rhys didn't know about the rest, and it was ugly. I also worried I might find something out that I didn't know. It felt as if a reckoning was right here in this room with us. Secrets were heavy, and I didn't want to keep someone else's secrets anymore.

"Archer?" my cousin prompted.

I held his gaze for several beats before taking a deep breath. "Are you sure you want to talk about this?"

"Yes, I am. I sense you know something I don't."

My heart thudded, and I tried to breathe slowly. "Okay, I know your granddad used to beat your brother."

"Yeah, that's not news," Rhys said bitterly. "He was rough with all of us, but he took more out on my brother. I always figured that was why Jake ended up drinking himself to death in college."

"I'm sure that was part of it," I agreed. "Look, are you sure you want me to tell you everything I know?"

"Just fucking tell me," he said flatly.

"Your granddad got rough with me a few times, but it was just physical. But the worst time was when it started—" I felt sick and had to swallow through the nausea and the bitter acid in my throat. "I walked in on him. He was with your brother in the office. I was ten at the time, so Jake was eleven."

"What the fuck was happening?"

"He was raping him." A strange sense of lightness slid through me as if saying the word out loud to someone other than my therapist instantly lifted the dark, heavy weight inside. The lightness didn't feel good. I literally felt light-headed with my brain buzzing and my chest tightening.

Rhys stopped his pacing. His mouth dropped open, and his eyes flew wide. "I'm sorry, what?"

"Your grandfather was raping Jake."

"Are you sure?"

"Yes. I don't want to get into the details, but I'm positive, and I hope you believe me." I still felt sick, but a sense of calm settled over me. I was simply speaking the truth.

The part that stood out the most powerfully was the look on Jake's face. It was as if part of him was checked out. Even though I didn't know this part with certainty, my gut told me what I saw wasn't the first time it had happened. There was a look of resignation on Jake's face, along with a blankness to his expression.

It was as if he had accepted it and was almost disconnected from the moment.

"Oh, my fucking god." Rhys stumbled as he stepped toward his desk chair, spinning it rapidly and plunking down on it.

"You didn't know this?" I asked.

He was deadly quiet for a moment, and then his breath came in heaves before he shook his head slowly. He met my eyes. "I did wonder, but I never saw it. Jake never told me. Oh, my fucking god."

"Are you okay?" I asked, reaching to rest my hand on his shoulder as I pushed away from the desk.

I let it fall when he straightened. "I'm okay if you're wondering if I can breathe."

We fell quiet, and I did an internal scan. I wasn't about to have a panic attack, which startled me.

"Oh, my fucking god," he repeated.

"I'm sorry," I said somberly.

He swallowed, the sound audible in the quiet office. "Obviously, you don't have anything to apologize for."

"I didn't have to tell you."

"It's not your secret to keep." He took a shaky breath and ran his hand through his hair. It fell with a thwack to his thighs. "Fuck. Does my grandfather know you know?"

"Yeah, he saw me. He hit me after that."

"Did you and Jake ever talk about it?"

"No, dude, I was ten. I'm pretty sure he preferred to forget it." I felt so helpless at that moment. "I just tried to be there for him. I knew he was reckless and drinking too much in college, but I didn't know what to do. I didn't know how to stop him. Obviously, I couldn't be with him all the time."

As I looked over at Rhys, my heart twisted sharply.

I felt awful. "You know, I've seen a therapist. It wouldn't hurt you to talk to somebody." Rhys stared at me and sagged into his chair. "He gives me fucking panic attacks. I've mostly gotten them under control, but it hasn't been easy."

"Shit. No wonder he hates you so much."

"Yeah, he knows I know something that could cause him a lot of trouble."

He sighed. "I'm guessing he also did more of these balloon loans. We're pressing legal charges. It's felony embezzlement," Rhys said firmly.

"You're sure you want to do that?"

"Hell yes. We can't charge him for what he did to my brother. Jake's dead. But he shouldn't get a pass on this."

"What about you? He used to beat you," I said flatly, almost startling myself with that comment.

Rhys shrugged. "I know, but I was a kid."

"Did he—?"

He shook his head slowly. "No, he didn't. My brother was always more his target. I thought it was because Jake was older."

"Shit." I let out a heavy sigh. "He's a fucking monster."

"More of a monster than I knew before."

"I'm sorry," I repeated.

"It's not your fault," Rhys said.

"Yeah, but I don't see how it helps you to know this."

"I want the truth. It helps me understand what Jake was going through."

"We need to talk to Gram together. Are we going to tell her this part?"

Rhys nodded. "I think we should. If we don't, I'm not sure she'll agree to press charges on the embezzlement. With this, she'll understand and want to do the one thing we can."

"All right, when do you want to talk to her?"

We both glanced at the clock on the wall. "Tomorrow. It's late. Let's go get a drink," he said.

Chapter Thirty-Four

PHOEBE

"He called?" My question came out in a screech.

My father nodded, his eyes worried. "Yes. He told us Archer can't help."

"Dad, I talked to Archer. I know he can help. Let me call him right now."

"I'm worried that will make it worse," my mother said.

"Mom, trust me, trust Archer. There's no way his uncle had the money to do that. Whatever he did was off the books."

I lifted my phone off the table, immediately calling Archer. Unfortunately, I got his voicemail.

"Hey, it's me. Clint called my parents and told them you can't help them with this. Please call me as soon as you get this. I miss you."

"I promise Archer will help," I said as soon as I hung up.

My mother let out a sigh. "This whole thing is stressful."

I made a sound of agreement. I wanted to tell them about Clint and his general awfulness, but I didn't know if I had permission. All I said was, "It'll be okay. I promise."

I finished coffee with my parents, worried that my father was just picking at his bagel. Later that evening, I finally heard back from Archer.

"I can help," he said as soon as I answered. "Clint's being an ass. Here's what's going on. He embezzled the money from the company to make the loan and is earning money off the payments. He didn't just do it with your parents, but other employees and former board members."

"Why is he threatening them?"

"I think he's upset because he doesn't have control of the company anymore. We're going to press charges. I've already talked to Rhys about it."

I sensed Archer wasn't telling me everything, but I didn't know why.

"How are you doing?" I asked.

"I'm okay. I'll need to stay a little longer because we're talking with the prosecutor and our attorneys, but I promise to keep you posted. Tell your parents not to take any more calls from him and to save any emails, messages, anything they hear from him."

"Of course. I'll talk to them right away."

"I miss you, Phoebe," he said, his voice low.

My throat felt tight, and my heart ached a little. "I miss you too."

I was starting to feel okay about it the next day. My parents promised they wouldn't answer any more calls from Clint.

My morning was routine until my phone rang. I recognized the area code for Seattle and answered, thinking it was Archer calling from his offices. My stomach dropped the moment I heard his great-uncle's voice.

"I'm going to keep this short and sweet. You need to tell your new husband to back the hell off. You also need to know he's lying to you."

"I'm not going to talk to you," I said firmly.

"Well, just listen."

Like an idiot, I did.

"He has secrets, big secrets, and he was tangled up in his cousin's death. If he keeps pushing on this, I'll expose the whole thing."

I made myself hang up. It was too late, though, because doubt started to churn in my gut. Archer's panic attacks, the way he always hedged whenever he talked about his uncle. Why was he hiding something from me?

When I felt my thoughts start to spin out into anxiety, I immediately tried to call Archer. I got his voicemail.

I decided to be direct. "Hey Archer, it's me. Can you call me as soon as you get this? Your uncle called me this time. I want to make sure you know what he said. I miss you."

After hanging up, I looked around the kitchen, shaking my head almost in wonder. The space was both familiar and new. The bones of the house remained the same, but it didn't feel the way it did all the hours I spent here when I was a little girl. The cool granite counter under my palm had once been a sunshiny yellow Formica. The new maple cabinets that brightened up the room when the sunlight came through the windows were once painted yellow with green trim.

Feeling jittery inside, I slid my hand over the

counter as I walked out. My socks were quiet on the hardwood floors in the hallway. There was no more plush carpet under my feet. I paused in the living room, memories bombarding me as I looked around. Archer's parents had set up a little play area for him in the corner. There'd been three bookcases that made it seem like a little room. I remembered when we made our science projects in first grade. His dad had helped us with the old volcano baking soda and vinegar thing. I'd wanted to make a replica of Mount Augustine, and Archer had made a replica of Mount Illiamna, two of the volcanoes in the Ring of Fire—the ring of volcanoes out in the Pacific Ocean near Alaska's coast.

Walking upstairs, I paused in the open area that was now his office. A sleek wooden desk faced the windows and not much else. I didn't have many memories of his parents' bedroom.

I suppose the door had been closed most of the time when I was here. I looked around, marveling that I was married to Archer. Lifting my hand, I admired the ring on my finger, whispering, "Wow."

This was my house, or so Archer kept saying. I didn't know what was happening, but he was gone just long enough that the rush and haze of falling in love was lifting. I needed to see him, and I needed to talk to him. Instead, I was worried about my father's balloon loan and Archer's great-uncle making threats.

Spinning on my heel, I decided to leave the house. I didn't need to be here alone, trapped in my thoughts.

Chapter Thirty-Five

ARCHER

My therapist, Marsha, smiled at me warmly. She studied me quietly for a moment before prompting, "Well, how do you feel about it?"

I rolled my eyes, letting out a sharp sigh. "I asked you how you felt about it."

"I know you did. And, of course, I have an opinion. But first I'd like to know how you feel. I want to make sure my opinion doesn't color what you think or feel."

I swallowed. "I should clarify. I don't want to tell my grandmother."

"When you say you don't want to tell her, what's behind that?" my therapist prompted gently.

"It's not my story to tell. But Jake's dead. It's confusing. Even though it didn't happen to me, somehow I'm ashamed." This secret had been heavy, and I felt tired of every emotion associated with it.

"Because what you saw carries a lot of shame with it," Marsha said softly but with a firm edge. "It's not your shame or Jake's. It's your great-uncle's."

I traced my fingertips over the fabric on the rounded armrest of the comfy chair. My therapist's office was comfortable and inviting. "Do you think he's ashamed?" I heard myself asking.

Marsha cocked her head to the side before lifting her shoulder in a slight shrug. "Perhaps. Research shows that many perpetrators do experience shame. They tend to mask it with anger and substance abuse. Very few people meet the criteria for being genuine sociopaths, meaning they have no empathy. I haven't met your great-uncle, but my speculation would be that he is not, solely based on how rare that is. He likely experiences some shame for his actions, which is why he lashes out with so much anger. In the end, you're here now, and your cousin isn't. I'm glad you told Rhys. Are you afraid of how Phoebe is going to respond if you tell her the whole story?"

"Of course, I mean..." Emotion throttled in my throat. I had to close my eyes and breathe through the sharp, abrupt pain. When I opened them, I saw zero judgment and nothing but warmth and understanding in my therapist's gaze. "I feel like I should have done something."

"You were ten years old," she said quietly. "Children are not responsible for the actions of the adults in their lives, and, Archer, you can't fix that. Please don't blame yourself. Anybody would understand that you weren't in a position to fix it." I swallowed again, hard. My chest finally started to loosen. "I think you should tell her. Because you love her. And it's a big part of your life and your story."

I groaned, leaning my elbows on my knees and running my hands through my hair when I straightened. I asked, "So what do you think?"

"I just told you what I think. I think it would help you to tell her. If I've learned one thing as a therapist, it's that when someone asks me if they should tell someone they love something, they probably should. The wondering about it is deep enough to drive a wedge between them if they don't. I don't mean you need to clear your conscience or anything like that. This is huge for you. It shaped your childhood. I've been treating you for panic attacks for two years, and you're doing so much better. This last detail is important."

"I told you this at the beginning," I said, feeling defensive.

"Oh, I didn't mean telling me. I mean facing what it means. Part of the reason your great-uncle is able to have such an effect on you is because this is still a secret. That gives the panic more power."

"Oh," I said slowly.

"Sure, he's going to say it's your word against his, but that's irrelevant. That's not the point."

"Are you always right?" I muttered, casting her a faux glare.

She smiled softly. "Definitely not."

"How do I tell her?"

"It won't be easy. It's an uncomfortable subject. This is why so many people keep things like this secret and why shame has so much power. How did it go with your cousin? Did he doubt you?"

"No," I said quickly.

"Phoebe won't either. She doesn't seem like the kind of person who would."

Marsha waited me out. That was a skill of hers I didn't particularly appreciate. After what had to be a full two minutes of silence, I said, "I'll tell her."

"I'm not saying you *have* to tell her."

"No, but I know you're right. I know that if I don't, it's always going to be there for me."

"How much longer are you in Seattle?" she asked

just as her friendly chime went off, letting us know our time was almost up.

"I was only supposed to be here a week, but with the embezzlement mess, I'll be here a little longer."

"Do you want to tell her in person?"

Chapter Thirty-Six

ARCHER

The truth rattled around in my heart and mind, and I finally settled on telling Phoebe over the phone. That way, if she freaked out, I would have some distance. The intellectual truth of the situation couldn't seem to override my jumbled emotions.

I called her as soon as I got her message. "What happened?"

"Clint called. He told me you're somehow responsible for Jake's death. I know it's all bullshit, but he's freaking me out."

"Oh, fuck," I muttered.

"What is he talking about, Archer? I know you didn't do anything," Phoebe pressed.

"No, I didn't. But I know something he doesn't want anyone to know. And I think the only way out of this is through it."

"What else haven't you told me?"

I opened my mouth to explain, but I stumbled on the words and ended up saying, "It's what I already told you. I promise I'll explain more, but let me talk to Rhys first."

I needed to talk to Rhys, and I needed to tell my family the ugly story, but I avoided telling Phoebe.

Fuck my life.

The mechanisms I'd developed to tolerate the anxiety and panic that flared were being stretched to their max. I wasn't on the verge of panic, but I knew if I had to confront Clint, I would be.

PHOEBE

"I wish I knew what was really happening," I finally said to Mae. Like me, Mae had recently moved back to Willow Brook, and we were getting together for coffee.

Mae nodded. "Well, family stuff is messy. Maybe what he's not telling you is someone else's to tell."

"Maybe."

"How are your parents holding up?"

"They're fine. My dad's embarrassed. I think that part is going to solve itself. I just hope Archer's great-uncle doesn't try to call them again. He's really an asshole."

"He sounds like a piece of work. If you need anything, say the word."

I didn't know how Mae could help, but it was good to have someone to listen. I was holding my worries at bay until I got another call from Clint. Good lord, the man knew how to leave an intimidating phone message. I didn't respond.

Then I showed up at work, and Graham called me into his office.

"Yes?" I looked over at him when I stepped into the office.

He gestured to the chair across from his desk. "Have a seat, and please close the door if you don't mind."

Oh, shit. I closed the door and sat down, smoothing my hands over my jeans. "Is everything okay?"

Graham studied me for a moment. "I don't know how to bring this up, but I got a strange call."

My belly turned. "Yeah?"

"I don't know if you're aware, but Fireweed Industries provides funding for some of our training and routinely funds an annual scholarship at the university in Anchorage to study wildfire mitigation. One of the family members contacted the university and shared concerns that if you remain here, they will withdraw the funding. I don't really know what's going on, but I thought I should alert you," he explained.

Dread was bitter and cold in my belly and crawled up my throat from my stomach. I opened my mouth to say I didn't even know what to think before shutting it and letting out a befuddled sigh.

"I don't know what to think. I don't know what this is about. I do know Archer is dealing with some family issues with his uncle. I promise you we won't lose the funding, but if it's a problem, I'll leave."

"I don't want you to leave," Graham said firmly. "I wanted you to know, and maybe you could follow up with Archer."

"Absolutely."

After I left Graham's office, I wanted to call Archer, but I didn't want to do it here at work. I called him in my car on the way home. His voice came through the speakers when he answered, "Hey, Phoebe. I'm glad you're calling."

"Hey, look, this is weird. Your uncle is now threatening to pull the funding from an annual scholarship related to wildfire mitigation. I guess it's funded through your family's business. Graham told me about it today."

"What?" Archer's question came out sharp. "That's, that's... What is...?" He stumbled over the words.

"Archer, please tell me what's going on." I didn't know anything, but I knew he was struggling. I could hear the threads of it in every word.

"Phoebe." Archer's voice went soft, and my heart twisted. He sounded a little lost. "Things are really getting messy here, and it's going to be longer than I planned."

"Archer, just tell me what's going on, please."

"I-I... I can't," he finally burst out.

The line went dead.

"Archer!" I exclaimed to myself alone in the car.

I tried calling him again, and he didn't answer. When I got home, I looked around the house that was supposed to start feeling like mine. Now, I couldn't even get him to tell me what was going on, and everything felt muddled. Part of me wanted to just say fuck it and not even try to do anything about this. But I was not going to let this go, not right now.

I lifted my phone and tapped on the video screen, quickly calling Archer. I almost burst into tears when he answered. I pressed my fingertips to the screen.

"Hey, thank you for answering," I said softly.

He nodded, his eyes holding mine through the magic of technology.

"Can you tell me what's happening?"

He was quiet for what felt like hours but was really probably maybe a minute. My heart hurt. Then he told me, and my heart felt broken open.

"Archer, oh, my god. Are you okay?"

"I'm fine, but it's all blowing up. I told my cousin. Between the embezzlement and this, I think Clint's just trying to find leverage wherever he can. I'm going to tell my parents and my grandmother and hope for the best. I have no idea what he's going to say to anybody."

He looked weary, and I wished I was there with him. "I need to go," he said abruptly.

"I love you," I said.

But the screen went blank.

Chapter Thirty-Eight

ARCHER

It felt as if a band was compressing my lungs. I forced myself to close my eyes and take a deep breath. This past week had been pure hell.

Clint knew I'd told Rhys and my grandmother what I saw. He was pitching a fit. Thankfully, for now, he was reduced to raging helplessly because he was facing charges connected to the embezzlement. The prosecutors were moving fast because we handed over the evidence from the company.

I hadn't handled that call with Phoebe well, and I knew it. "Fuck," I muttered.

I stood from my desk and paced in a tight circle. Crossing to the windows, I looked out across Puget Sound. The fog was rolling in, creating layers of gray from the ocean's surface and blending into the sky. This place that had never felt like home, and now it felt even less like home. I'd been born in Alaska and grown up there.

As I paced back and forth in front of the windows, the tightness started to ease inside. For the first time all week, it occurred to me I hadn't actually had a panic attack this week.

"Fuck, that's crazy."

"What's crazy?" My cousin's voice came from the doorway.

Turning, I stopped pacing, a surprised laugh bubbling up. I shrugged. "This week hasn't been as bad as I thought."

Rhys walked into my office, closing the door behind him. "How the hell can that be? It's been fucking hell for me."

"Oh, it's been hell all right. I just—" I hesitated before deciding to be honest. "I haven't had a panic attack all week. Usually, I have them when I have to deal with your grandfather. I think maybe having it all out there has taken some weight off."

Rhys plunked down in one of the chairs across from my desk, letting out a ragged sigh. He ran both of his hands through his hair and let his arms fall. "I guess that would help. Fuck, man, I wish I'd known sooner."

I rounded my desk and sat down in the chair situated at an angle across from his. "We were just kids. I'm fucking stressed to the max. It's just I'm not losing it, and that's a relief."

We fell quiet. Rhys rested his elbows on his knees, angling to glance at me. "What's your plan?"

"What do you mean?"

"Do you plan to live here in Seattle or in Alaska?"

I didn't even hesitate. "Alaska. I'll travel here whenever I need to for work, but that's home for me." He nodded before I added, "You know we don't have to have these offices here."

"What?" He straightened, leaning back as his brows hitched up. "What do you mean?"

"When I told my parents this whole mess, my dad explained it was your grandfather who rented this space. They said he wanted something outside of Alaska. You always said you preferred to be home in Fireweed Harbor."

Rhys laughed softly. "There's so much I don't fucking know. This location costs us a fortune."

"No shit. Go back to Fireweed Harbor and stay."

"I just might. I can travel if I need to, but without these offices, I probably won't need to that often."

"You call that therapist?" I asked.

He shook his head quickly. I knew he wasn't ready. "I will. Maybe." When I arched a brow, he added, "All right. I promise I'll think about it."

We hadn't spoken at length about what I'd shared with him, but it was obviously weighing on him.

"You talk to Phoebe?" he lobbed my way.

I winced, and Rhys cocked his head. "What?"

"I didn't handle it too well."

"You'll get through it. She's the real deal. I knew it as soon as I saw you two together."

I prayed he was right. I glanced at my watch. "You want to go grab dinner?"

"Can we agree not to talk about my grandfather?"

"Absolutely."

Later that night when I tried to call Phoebe, she didn't answer.

Chapter Thirty-Nine

PHOEBE

I adjusted my bag strap on my shoulder and hurried off the plane. No matter how smoothly a flight went, it always ended with feeling jostled. The seats were crowded. There was a crying baby to one side, which I preferred to the drunk guy on the other side, and the jerk arguing with the flight attendant in the row in front of me.

I'd decided to fly to Seattle to see Archer. I wanted to be there for him face-to-face and kick the doubts crowding my mind to the curb. I'd planned poorly, though. As soon as I walked out of the airport, I realized I didn't even know where his office was. I whipped out my phone to bring up Fireweed Industries online. Of course, the address listed was where the company was founded in Fireweed Harbor, where Archer's parents lived now.

I searched for the Seattle address and got a post office box. Fuck. I'd wanted to surprise him. I caved and finally replied to his text.

Me: *Hey, where are you?*

Archer: *In Seattle. I missed your voice last night.*

Me: *I need your address.*

I was still going to try to surprise him. Unfortunately, he knew me way too well. I wasn't one for being all vague, and he obviously noticed.

Archer: *Are you at the airport?*

I sighed.

Me: *Yes.*

Archer: *I'll be there in twenty minutes. Tell me where you're waiting.*

I glanced around, my eyes landing on a sign.

Me: *I'm right outside baggage claim in the pickup zone for the car services.*

Archer: *Stand where I can see you. I'm on the way. I love you.*

For the first time since he left Willow Brook, my tension eased. I was exhausted, having hardly slept because I'd flown during the night, but it would be okay because I was about to see Archer. He arrived almost exactly twenty minutes later.

I stood on the curb while I waited, realizing I should have asked him what he would be driving. A moment later, a black SUV pulled up to the curb. It matched his vehicle in Alaska. He was out in a flash, rounding the SUV to me.

"Phoebe, what the hell are you doing here?" he asked, his concerned gaze skating over my face.

"You're going through a lot, and I wanted to see you," I said firmly.

My throat tightened with emotion as his eyes searched mine. He pulled me into a fierce hug, and I squeezed him close. A moment later, I stepped back. Peering up, I asked, "How are you?"

His lips curled into a small, bemused smile. "Better now that you're here. Let's talk on the drive."

A few minutes later, he drove out of the airport

pickup area, I glanced over. He was wearing slacks and a button-down shirt.

"Wow, you're all business-y," I offered.

"This is what I wear when I'm in Seattle, but good news. We're closing down these offices." He cast me a quick smile before looking back at the road.

"You are? Why is that good news?"

"Because..." He paused, letting out a sigh. "I have a lot to catch you up on."

"I know, but tell me about the offices. That's probably the boring part," I said softly, my heart twisting a little to think of what he'd been dealing with.

"I guess so. When I told my parents everything—" His eyes slid to mine, and I nodded encouragingly. "My dad filled me in on more background. My great-uncle is the one who insisted on opening the offices in Seattle. The business started in Fireweed Harbor, the place where my parents live now. According to my dad, Clint wanted something in the city. It's a waste of money, so I talked to Rhys, and we're closing this location down, but I'll take you on the tour."

"How soon will you close this location?"

"We'll do it gradually and probably keep a small office here just for meetings, but that's it. With the online options, we don't need a footprint in Seattle," he explained as he drove, weaving expertly through the traffic. "The business started as a vineyard, and that's our primary business. We expanded into a number of other ventures, including mining in areas where we owned the rights. But we closed most of those down over the last decade. The only one left is the one I'm closing in Willow Brook or rather, preventing from being reopened."

"Have you decided what to do?"

"We're transitioning our plant to renewable energy.

It's going to take some work, but we'll manage. I'll be juggling the planning with Rhys. Here's to hoping the family dynamics don't get too messy."

"What do you mean?" While Archer and I had done a lot of catching up with each other, we hadn't talked at length about his planning with the business in his new role. We simply hadn't had the time yet, and in all honesty, we had focused on the personal aspect of reconnecting.

"Well, including Rhys and me, eight of us stand to inherit various portions of the business. Rhys has six younger siblings."

"Oh, wow. You mentioned you had a lot of cousins. I guess I never realized they were all connected through him."

"Yeah, it's a lot. For now, I'm going to focus on the renewable energy, and he's going to focus on the vineyards. We'll figure the rest out from there. You want to take a look at the offices?" he asked as he took an exit off the highway that led straight into downtown Seattle.

"Only if you want me to."

"Let me stop by. I need to grab my laptop and close up."

I followed Archer up to his office, commenting, "Ooh, fancy-schmancy," as we walked through the sleek, modern space. He grinned.

"Oh, you have a beautiful view."

The sun was starting to set over Puget Sound, a watercolor of tangerine and gold shimmering on the ocean's surface and staining the sky.

"I do. I love this view," he commented as he closed his laptop and slid it with some papers into a small shoulder bag.

"Will you miss it?" I asked.

His head whipped up, that familiar silver-smoke gaze meeting mine. He paused before replying, "Yes and no."

"What do you mean?"

"I missed Willow Brook a lot more than I'll miss this." He rounded the desk, catching my hands in his as he took a step back, resting his hips on the desk and pulling me between his knees.

"Really?" I asked.

He smoothed a loose lock of hair off my cheek, sending hot shivers chasing through me when his fingertips brushed over the shell of my ear. "Really." His eyes held mine, the look there so intimate, my breath caught in my throat. "I kind of rushed off the video call the other night."

"It's okay. I know it wasn't easy to tell me."

I pressed a kiss on his cheek before leaning back and studying him. "I'm so sorry for what happened. I don't like knowing it's just... it's you, and it's me, and—"

"It's us," he whispered gruffly.

Emotion rushed through me as I nodded. "I don't want there to be secrets, and it helps me understand a lot. This is big. It must have been hard for you this week."

His shoulders rose as he took a deep breath, falling when he let it out in a sigh. "It's been hell, but I haven't had a single panic attack."

"Wow." I squeezed his hand.

"Don't get me wrong, I've been fucking stressed. My anxiety has been pretty bad at times, but I think the secret played into my panic. Now it's just out there, and everybody who matters knows. Has Clint called you again?"

I shook my head quickly. "No, not—"

"Since yesterday," Archer finished my sentence. At my nod, he took a quick breath. "Rhys and I went together and told my grandmother. I told my parents, and he's already been notified they're pressing charges on the embezzlement. I don't know what he thought he was going to make up about me, but he's backed way the hell off."

"I don't like him," I said stoutly.

"Join the club." His tone was as dry as chalk and laced with bitterness.

"Do you want to talk about it?" I asked carefully.

He shook his head. "No, I'm pretty talked out for now."

"I'm here if you need to talk."

He leaned forward, pressing a kiss to my lips. "I know. Why don't we go have dinner?"

"Do we have to go out?" I asked.

"Not if you don't want to. Tell me your favorite food, and we'll get takeout. I know all the best places."

Chapter Forty

EPILOGUE

Archer

Two weeks later

As I stepped through the automatic doors at the airport in Anchorage, a blast of cold air struck my cheeks. Phoebe shivered, glancing up and commenting, "It's March, and it's still freezing."

I smiled. "I don't care. Plus, we're taking that mud season vacation soon."

She laughed and reached for my hand. An hour or so later, we were walking into our house. I loved thinking of it as *our* house. It represented my life with her. I'd gone back to my past to find my future. What I wanted to be only a week-long trip to Seattle had turned into three, but Phoebe had stayed with me.

We'd covered a lot of territory as far as planning our lives. She was seriously considering how long she'd continue with hotshot firefighting. I loved that she loved her job, but I'd have been lying through my teeth if I said I wouldn't worry about her. It was a risky job.

We wanted time together because we'd missed a lot over the years. For now, she'd committed to the next season, and we'd go from there. I'd talked through the planning for primarily working in Willow Brook with occasional travel to Fireweed Harbor and Seattle.

Later that night, we were in the kitchen. Phoebe had insisted on trying to make a pizza in our new oven, which had a wood-burning section.

"That smells like an amazing test case. How long do we have to wait?"

She glanced at the clock on the oven. "Fifteen minutes."

I waggled my eyebrows. "Plenty of time."

"Archer." She rolled her eyes. "You're ridiculous."

"Come'ere," I said, catching her hand where she stood at the end of the kitchen island. I reeled her to me, spinning on my stool to pull her between my knees.

"What?" she asked.

"This." I fit my mouth over hers.

I kept thinking my need for her would start to abate, but it was always right there on the edge. My body was like dry tinder, and Phoebe the spark. The second her tongue tangled with mine, I groaned and slid my hand down her back. Giving her lush bottom a nice squeeze, I loved how she squeaked in my mouth and pulled back with a startled laugh.

"I'm cooking!"

"No, you're not. The oven's doing all the work now."

It wasn't difficult to persuade Phoebe after I kissed her again and teased between her thighs. Fiery minutes burned by before I turned her and bent her over the counter. She pleaded, "Archer, please."

Being with Phoebe like this was home for my body, my heart, and my soul. Of course, I made sure she flew first, and then my own release shook me to my core. I could barely stand and thanked the gods I had the counter to hold on to, along with the sweet curve of her hip.

After we untangled ourselves, she turned and gave me a sassy smile. "You're too much."

"Never."

Want a glimpse of the future for Archer & Phoebe? Join my newsletter to receive an exclusive scene:

Sign up here: https://BookHip.com/FKWVNDR

p.s. If you are already subscribed, you'll still be able to access the scene.

Thank you for reading Archer & Phoebe's story - I hope you loved it!

Up next in the Light My Fire Series is Hallie & Chase's story. Hallie's looking for an escape. Just for one night. No last names, no phone numbers.

Chase gives her exactly what she needs, and they never expect to see each other again. Until Hallie discovers she's pregnant.

She only has one way to find the man who she thought would be nothing but a memory.

Don't miss Chase & Hallie's story - it's hot, emotional. Chase is just the protective hero you need!

Pre-order Keep Me Close - due out June 28, 2022!

For more swoony romance...

This Crazy Love kicks off the Swoon Series - small town southern romance with enough heat to melt you! Jackson & Shay's story is epic - swoon-worthy & intensely emotional. Jackson just happens to be Shay's brother's best friend. He's also *seriously* easy on the eyes. Shay has a past, the kind of past she would most definitely like to forget. Past or not, Jackson is about to rock her world. Don't miss their story! Free on all retailers!

Burn For Me is a second chance romance for the ages. Sexy firefighters? Check. Rugged men? Check. Wrapped up together? Check. Brave the fire in this hot, small-town romance. Amelia & Cade were high school sweethearts & then it all fell apart. When they cross paths again, it's epic - don't miss Cade's story! Free on all retailers!

For more small town romance, take a visit to Last Frontier Lodge in Diamond Creek. A sexy, alpha SEAL meets his match with a brainy heroine in Take Me Home. Marley is all brains & Gage is all brawn. Sparks fly when their worlds collide. Don't miss Gage & Marley's story!
Free on all retailers!

If sports romance lights your spark, check out The Play. Liam is a British footballer who falls for Olivia, his doctor. A twist of forbidden heats up this swoon-worthy & laugh-out-loud romance. Don't miss Liam & Olivia's story.

Free on all retailers!

Light My Fire Series
Wild With You
Hold Me Now
Only Ever Us
Fall For Me
Keep Me Close - coming June 2022!
Dare With Me Series
Crash Into You
Evers & Afters
Come To Me
Back To Us
Take Me There - coming May 2022!
Swoon Series
This Crazy Love
Wait For Me
Break My Fall
Truly Madly Mine
Still Go Crazy
If We Dare
Steal My Heart
Into The Fire Series
Burn For Me
Slow Burn
Burn So Bad
Hot Mess
Burn So Good
Sweet Fire
Play With Fire
Melt With You
Burn For You
Crash & Burn
That Snowy Night
Brit Boys Sports Romance
The Play
Big Win

Out Of Bounds
Play Me
Naughty Wish
Diamond Creek Alaska Novels
When Love Comes
Follow Love
Love Unbroken
Love Untamed
Tumble Into Love
Christmas Nights
Last Frontier Lodge Novels
Take Me Home
Love at Last
Just This Once
Falling Fast
Stay With Me
When We Fall
Hold Me Close
Crazy For You
Just Us

RESOURCES

Archer's story involves the trauma caused by witnessing a traumatic event, in addition to experiencing physical abuse by a family member. Child abuse is more common than many understand, and the emotional and psychological pain and shame that victims carry can be devastating. If you or anyone you know has experienced abuse or assault, there are resources for help.

National Center for Victims of Crime: www.victimsofcrime.org
1-202-467-8700

National Sexual Assault Hotline: http://www.thehotline.org
1-656-4673 (HOPE)

. . .

National Sexual Assault Online Hotline: https://ohl.
rainn.org/online/

ACKNOWLEDGMENTS

I'm forever grateful to you, my readers, for reading my stories and giving me the motivation to keep writing them - thank you!!!

Gracious thanks to my editor and to Terri D. for proofreading and making sure my timelines make sense. Did you know there can be more than one Wednesday in a single week? #authorproblems

Najla Qamber created another beautiful cover, and I'm so thankful for her work and her patience with me. If you ever wondered, cover design is ***not*** one of my talents.

Much appreciation to my early readers who catch the stubborn errors, and to the bloggers who spread the word about my stories.

As always, my husband gives me the time and space to write. Our dogs nap by my desk and make sure I get enough exercise.

xoxo

J.H. Croix

ABOUT THE AUTHOR

USA Today Bestselling Author J. H. Croix lives in a small town in Maine with her husband and three spoiled dogs. Croix writes contemporary romance with sassy women and alpha men who aren't afraid to show some emotion. Her love for quirky small-towns and the characters that inhabit them shines through in her writing. Take a walk on the wild side of romance with her bestselling novels!

Places you can find me:
jhcroixauthor.com
jhcroix@jhcroix.com

facebook.com/jhcroix

instagram.com/jhcroix

bookbub.com/authors/j-h-croix